WALK THE LINE

J. KENNER

Walk The Line

by

J. Kenner

About Walk The Line

Elena is too young for me, not to mention she's my boss's daughter and my babysitter.

That's beyond complicated. And I'm not even looking for a relationship—but I can't deny the attraction that sizzles between us.

I need to ignore it. A single dad, all I want is to take care of my little girl, do my job, and enjoy my friends. Anything more is asking for complications I can't afford. Asking to be hurt again.

Trouble is, I want her, too. And when our flirty sparks turn to flames, I give in to temptation. Our secret fling is scorching hot, better than I'd even imagined.

But secrets get out, and I could lose my job and my reputation.

And I'm starting to realize she's the one thing I'm not willing to lose.

Each book in the series is a STANDALONE with NO cliffhanger and a guaranteed HEA!

But even so, you won't want to miss any in the series. Because then you can answer the question…

Who's Your Man of the Month?

Down On Me
Hold On Tight
Need You Now
Start Me Up
Get It On
In Your Eyes
Turn Me On
Shake It Up

All Night Long
In Too Deep
Light My Fire
Walk The Line

and don't miss Bar Bites: A Man of the Month Cookbook!

Chapter One

ELENA ANDERSON HURRIED up Austin's Congress Avenue on autopilot, dodging pedestrians, street musicians, and a cluster of middle school kids being herded by a harried looking teacher and a few stressed-out chaperones.

She swerved in and out of the post-lunch crowds, then breathed a sigh of relief when she finally turned east on Sixth Street. Just a few more blocks and she could deliver her news. Though she still wasn't certain if it was the good news or the bad news that was driving her forward motion.

With a sigh, she slowed her pace slightly, thinking about what had happened—and what she'd learned. An opportunity for her dad and his bar,

The Fix on Sixth. And a missed opportunity for her.

Wasn't there some saying about life being a teeter-totter? Her dad was going up, but her boss had just sent her crashing down.

"Get over it, girl," she told herself, too loudly apparently, since a nearby woman in killer heels eyed her curiously.

She flashed the woman a smile and stepped up her pace again, so that she was breathless when she tugged open the heavy oak door that led into The Fix on Sixth.

Hard to believe that it had only been a few months since she'd left San Diego to come to Austin and find her father. Harder still to believe that for most of her twenty-three years she and her mother had believed him to be dead, the result of a horrible deception played out by Elena's grandfather who hadn't thought that Tyree was good enough for his daughter, Eva.

Elena had been so angry when she'd learned the truth. Angry at her grandfather. Angry at the world. And, yes, even angry at her mother and Tyree for not somehow magically discovering the truth and overcoming all the barriers that had been tossed between them.

She'd wallowed in that anger for a while, but it was uncomfortable and constraining, like wearing a dress that fit too tight. On the whole, she was an upbeat person, and that anger bubbling up from the past fizzled quickly away, replaced by what her mother always called her indelible optimism.

Back then, she'd known little more than Tyree Johnson's name and the fact that he'd served in the Navy. But the Internet is a wondrous thing, and she'd lost herself in search engines, following rabbit trail after rabbit trail until she'd finally found an article about a Tyree Johnson opening a bar in Austin, Texas. There'd been a picture, and she'd recognized him right away from the tattered snapshot she'd had from birth. A picture of her father that Eva had kept in Elena's crib, ensuring that she'd always be close to the father she could never know.

Except she could know him.

And now, thanks to the Internet and persistence, she *did* know him.

She'd come to Austin with the dream of finding her

father and getting to know him. And, yes, she'd hoped that romance would brew again between Tyree and Eva. She believed in happily ever afters, after all. But she hadn't held her breath, and she'd told herself that all she wanted was a chance to know her father.

Now here she was. Her dad and mom were engaged, Elena had a half-brother who was a great kid, and she'd already become close with her dad, so much so that it felt like they had years of history and not just months.

So, yeah. Things worked out. She just needed to remember that. She'd find a better job; this wasn't a crisis, it was an opportunity. And she was going to help Tyree do everything necessary to solidify The Fix as Austin's premier local bar.

At two in the afternoon, the bar wasn't very crowded. A few customers were scattered at tables, but she barely noticed them as she stepped inside.

She did, however, immediately notice Brent. How could she not? He was, hands down, the most handsome man she'd ever seen. He had an athlete's body —tall and lean, with broad shoulders and chiseled arms. She'd never seen his bare chest, but she'd seen him enough in the black *The Fix on Sixth* logo t-shirt to imagine the taut muscles of his chest and abs. He had a strong face and whiskey-brown eyes that were quick to laugh, and the depth of love that she saw on his face when he looked at his five-year-old daughter always gave Elena butterflies.

She wanted him to look at her that way.

But no. That was *not* the direction she needed her thoughts to go. She hadn't even launched into her career, and she had no interest in getting tied down. Especially not with a single dad. He was settled. She craved adventures. She had two years of grad school in Austin in front of her, and then who knew where she might land? With the career she'd chosen —urban planning—she could work almost anywhere. Even Europe, and wouldn't that be exciting?

And while she couldn't deny that a fling with that man would be amazing, she knew damn well that wouldn't happen. For one, although she felt all kinds of sparks when she was near him, he'd shown no interest in her except as a friend. For another, he was a full ten years older than her. Or, nine, actually, since she'd turn twenty-four next week. But that was still a big gap, especially since Brent was one of Tyree's closest friends, and how awkward was that?

No. She needed to keep her distance and her wits. A crush was okay, so long as he didn't realize she had one. Which he wouldn't, because she could hide her feelings just fine.

"What's wrong?" Brent asked, looking up as she hurried into The Fix.

Then again, maybe she couldn't hide her feelings at all.

Her stomach did a flip-flop simply from the sound of his voice, but she ignored it, her attention going first to her father. "I need to talk to you. And to you," she added to Brent, hoping she seemed casual and business-like. "It's about the bar and the historical commission, and it's important." She rattled off the words, looking at both their faces.

"Of course," Brent said, shooting a glance toward Tyree. "We can talk right now."

He signaled for Jenna and Reece to follow, and Elena gave herself a mental whack on the head. She'd zeroed in on Brent so quickly she hadn't even noticed his two best friends.

She didn't know the whole story, of course, but

apparently Jenna and Reece and Brent had been friends since they were kids. Only it turned out that Reece and Jenna had secret crushes on each other —crushes that weren't so secret now that Jenna's pregnancy was showing.

Elena also hadn't noticed Griffin and Beverly when she'd hurried into the bar, but now she saw them sitting together, half-watching her, but mostly looking at each other. They looked surprisingly cozy, which made her smile—she knew that Bev had been attracted to Griffin for months, but Griffin did a good job of keeping his emotions to himself.

A burn victim, Griffin had been horribly scarred as a child. Elena had learned as much not long after she'd come to The Fix. She'd also learned how much he closed himself off and kept his scars covered.

Beverly, on the other hand, was a movie star, and absolutely gorgeous. Elena had to admit that she'd been doubtful that the two would ever get together. And although she'd never been happier to be wrong, she couldn't deny the unwelcome twinge of envy that cut through her—because she was damn sure that Brent would never surprise her in the same way.

She shook her head, banishing the thoughts, then shot Beverly a quick smile as she followed the men and Jenna into the back office.

"All right, *mon bijou*," Tyree said, his Cajon roots showing in the nickname he'd recently started calling her. He was leaning against his desk, his brow furrowed with worry. He was a big man, his skin as dark as hers, though that's about all she inherited from him. She had her mother's build and high cheekbones, not to mention her wide eyes. And now that Elena wore her hair short, mother and daughter looked almost like sisters.

Tyree had never said as much, but she knew that he'd been doubtful when she'd stepped into The Fix. He probably assumed she was David's kid. But David Anderson had married Eva after Tyree was killed in action. Or, at least, after Eva had believed as much.

Elena didn't remember David—the marriage had been arranged by Elena's grandfather, and Eva had finally divorced him when Elena was four—so Tyree was the only father she knew. She'd missed a lot, but it made this new time between them extra special.

And she really loved the nickname.

"What's going on?" Tyree continued. "You look about to burst with news, but I can't tell if it's good or bad."

"Mostly bad for me," Elena said. "But good for you. Or at least potentially good," she said with a shrug.

She saw Brent and Reece exchange quick glances as Tyree pushed off from the desk, the furrows deepening. "Bad for you how?"

"It's okay," she said, regretting that she'd spoken out of turn. "Really, I shouldn't have said anything. What I came to talk to you about is what I overheard."

Tyree looked like he was going to press the point, but Brent nodded to one of the chairs, indicating that she should sit. "Go ahead and tell us," he said. "You said it involved The Fix and the historical commission?"

"Right." She sat, her hands on her knees as she gathered her thoughts. "Okay, so you know I was working for the Austin Center for Downtown Conservation and Revitalization, right?"

"Was?" Brent repeated, because the man never missed a beat.

A second later Tyree took a step toward her, concern etched in his kind eyes. "Elena? What happened?"

She looked pointedly at them both. "Hold on. I'm getting there." She saw Brent's mouth twitch with amusement and told herself that she needed to not look at him if she was going to get through the story. The man was far too distracting.

"They called me in this morning—well, Cecily did. She's the woman I've been reporting to, and she said that they were so impressed with my work and that she thinks I'll go far in the business. Which was great to hear, but I could tell the meeting wasn't just about complimenting me."

She broke her own rule and glanced at Brent, who was looking at her intently. "Anyway," she continued, "after a few minutes of that, she told me that their board of directors had met recently and that times being what they were, that they were going to have to cut my position."

"Oh, sugar," Tyree said. "I'm so sorry."

"They assured me they wanted to keep me on, but said it just wasn't possible. But they did write a killer letter of recommendation." She sighed. All things considered, she'd rather have the job. "At any rate," she continued before they started throwing pity at her, "while I was clearing out some of my stuff, I overheard the conversation in the next room."

She glanced around, her eyes bouncing off of Brent and locking on her father. "The Center's just a nonprofit organization, but they work closely with the city, and apparently there's a push to raise awareness of the history of Sixth Street. Apparently a lot of folks don't even know that it used to be called Pecan Street. They're talking about asking businesses in historic buildings to offer tours and maybe host artifacts or hand out leaflets about the history of the area."

"That sounds like a good program," Jenna said. She was already seated in one of the chairs, her hand protectively over her belly.

"I thought so, too," Elena said, then turned to face Tyree. "And I also thought that we could take a lead. Now that I know it's coming, if we go ahead and start doing some of that, then not only might it mean extra publicity for the bar, but we'll end up being leaders in the campaign to increase historical awareness.

"I'm sure they'll put together some sort of committee," she added. "We show early that we're interested in the cause and you'll probably end up on their radar to be part of the core planning group. You could even approach them and let them know you want to raise awareness. Maybe see if they have some sort of plaque. Just to get the dialogue going, you know?"

She glanced around at all the faces. "I know that this kind of thing is more exciting to me than it is to you. But it's not just about the planning. I think it could really up The Fix's reputation in the city."

Tyree and Reece exchanged glances, then Tyree nodded. "This is all excellent information," he said. "Considering how much our income has spiked since we started the Man of the Month contest, I think it's fair to say that we won't be going out of business any time soon."

"Which means it makes sense to get involved," Jenna said. "And tossing historical tidbits into the mix makes a lot of sense. We could ask Spencer and Brooke to throw in a few facts during the last episode of *The Business Plan*. And we're already taking a leadership role in the downtown area with the food fair."

"That's true," Elena said. When she'd first arrived in Austin, the bar just launched the Man of the Month contest, a calendar guy contest that had been created in the hopes of drawing more business to The Fix, and thereby keeping it solvent and in business.

The contest had succeeded beyond anyone's expectations, and now there was no question that when Tyree's December thirty-first deadline came, The Fix would be solidly in the black.

Riding on that success, everyone at the bar had been thinking about how to keep The Fix in the public eye, and the idea of a food fair had come up. Jenna had jumped into planning, and now the date was growing closer, with dozens of Austin's restaurants and specialty food stores signed up to participate. And since The Fix was the founder and organizer, the bar's name would be all over the Winston Hotel ballroom the night of the fair.

Tyree moved to stand in front of her. "I appreciate everything you're suggesting, and I'm sure not disagreeing. But you haven't mentioned what you're going to do." His voice was gentle, but he wore a no-nonsense expression.

"Me?"

"You quit your job here to work at the Center. What are you doing for income?"

"Daddy…"

Tyree's serious expression softened, replaced by a wide, shining grin. "I do like the way that sounds."

She rolled her eyes, but that was only for show. Because she liked the way it sounded, too. And they both knew it.

She reached out, and soon her hand was engulfed in her father's larger one.

"I'm going to look for something else, of course. And they said they might bring me on as an intern. But I guess that's something they have to clear with the board, too. So I'm in a holding pattern."

"An intern," Tyree repeated. "You mean unpaid."

"There's value in the experience," she said, but he only exhaled. Loudly.

"Why don't you come back to work here? I don't have a lot of hours available, but we do have one part-time slot to fill."

Elena almost sagged with relief. She hadn't wanted to seem presumptuous and ask, but she really did need the work.

But just as she was about to jump all over Tyree's offer, Jenna let out a low sigh from behind Elena. "I'm so sorry," she said, moving to stand by Brent. "I hired someone this morning."

Tyree's brow furrowed. "We haven't even posted the position yet."

Jenna waved his words away with a curt, "She'd called me last week. I know her. It was one of those things. Anyway," she continued, rushing on, "just because there's nothing here doesn't mean you're out of luck. After all, you need a babysitter, right?" As she spoke, she nudged Brent with her shoulder. "Didn't that new girl you'd hired just quit? And now that you have to work weekends, it makes sense. Don't you think so, Elena?"

Her heart did a back-flip at the prospect, and her head immediately cringed. Honestly, what was she thinking? Work for Brent? Close quarters? Late nights? His house? His daughter?

Granted he'd hardly ever be there, but even so, that was a recipe for disaster. Or, at least, for embarrassing herself.

She had to say no.

"I really could use you," Brent said, his casual words conjuring all sorts of delicious images.

"Oh," Elena said, not even sure if he could hear her over the wild pounding of her heart. "In that case, yes."

Chapter Two

"HE SAID he could use you? My, my, my." Selma Herrington sat cross-legged on Elena's living room floor, her choppy, ever-changing hair tipped with pink today. She grinned as she shot a glance toward Hannah Donovan, a local attorney who was dating Matthew Herrington, Selma's brother.

"As a *babysitter*," Elena said, feeling her cheeks warm.

"But you want more, right?" Hannah asked. "I mean, you've been attracted to Brent since day one."

A quick jolt of panic shot through Elena, because that was a fact she'd been working hard to keep hidden from the man herself. She'd told no one but

Selma, and only then in a weak moment in the back room of The Fix when they'd been talking about life and men and movies while Selma restocked the whiskey.

Elena and Selma had hit it off quickly. Elena had been new in town, The Fix her only real home base. Selma owned a whiskey distillery, and as one of the bar's suppliers, she'd been a steady figure in The Fix from the day Elena had walked through the doors.

They'd started out as casual acquaintances then worked their way up to friends. Not hard with Selma, who was quirky enough to be interesting and genuine enough to be likable.

Now, however, Elena was reviewing that assessment, and she shot her friend a WTF glance. Immediately, Selma raised her hands in defense. "I didn't say a word until she asked."

Elena's attention went to Hannah, who looked a little sheepish. "I've seen you looking at Brent the same way I looked at Matthew before he looked back." Her smile suggested all kinds of intimate secrets. "I guess I just hoped."

"Oh, God. Was I really that obvious?"

"Only to another woman," Selma said. "Seriously, Brent's clueless. But maybe that's part of the problem," she added with a trill to her voice.

"There is no problem," Elena said firmly.

"Oh, please. You aren't banging him. That sounds like a problem."

"Selma!"

"Just saying what we're all thinking."

"I'm not interested in him that way. Or," she added before either of the woman could challenge that statement, "I'm not naive enough to think that he's interested in me. And even if he were, it's *so* not going to happen."

"Why not?" Hannah said. "If you're interested and he's interested..." She trailed off with a shrug, her tone suggesting all sorts of naughty things.

"Because I'm still in grad school, and he's a divorced father. He has a life. I have a tuition bill. He's worried about Faith's college fund, and I haven't even begun my career."

Hannah and Selma exchanged glances. "All legitimate concerns," Selma said. "All surmountable."

Elena shook her head in exasperation. "You guys are impossible. Are we getting food or not?"

They'd made plans for a Saturday morning break-fast earlier in the week, intending to meet at Elena's place and then head out to one of Austin's many Tex-Mex dives for migas. But they'd gotten side-tracked by Elena's love life, or lack thereof. Now, her stomach was complaining as much as her libido was.

Hannah looked at her watch. "We're never going to find a place without a line. What have you got in the apartment? Wanna just stay in and cook?"

"Sure," Elena said, rising. Back in California, she hadn't been much of a cook. But once she moved here, she started hanging out at her dad's house and cooking with him and Eli, her half-brother. "Actu-ally, I think I have everything for migas." A mix of scrambled eggs, onions, tomatoes, Serrano peppers, sour cream, and tortilla chips, the Tex-Mex break-fast was a favorite. "I have salsa and tortillas, too. All we're missing is the atmosphere."

"And someone to wait on us," Hannah pointed out.

"Who cares, as long as we still get the migas?" Selma said. "Besides, I'm much more generous where Mimosas are concerned. Do you have cham-pagne?" she added as an afterthought. "And orange juice for that matter."

"Strangely, I do."

"Your kitchen is better stocked than mine," Selma said. "Easton and I both hate grocery shopping. We have take-out containers and whiskey. Lots of whiskey."

"Ours is mostly fruit and protein," Hannah said. "I love your brother," she added to Selma, "but the guy eats too well. Although he does have a weakness for Mrs. Johnson's donuts."

"Well, who doesn't?" Selma added.

An Austin favorite since the forties, Mrs. Johnson's Bakery had some of the best donuts Elena had ever tasted. Seriously, California had the beach, but Austin had a hell of a lot going for it. Including her family. And Brent.

"Come on," she said, heading toward the kitchen. "You guys can sit at the bar and we can continue this while I cook. Or we could change topics?" she added, but without much hope.

"The hell with that," Selma said as she followed. "I

want all the details of today. You're going when? And what time is he coming home?"

Elena frowned as she pulled a carton of eggs out of the fridge. "I'm going over to his place at four. I think he'll be back home around three in the morning. And why does that matter?"

"You'll see him coming and going," Selma said.

"And you can ask Faith about him," Hannah added.

Elena paused on the way back to the fridge to gape at her friend. "I am not hitting up a five-year-old for information on the guy I'm crushing on."

Hanna and Selma exchanged significant glances. "At least she's admitting the crush," Hannah said.

"I never denied it. You guys are just pulling my chain now."

"Maybe a little," Hannah admitted.

"Well, stop it. I'm already stressed out enough simply from the idea of working that close to him."

"Except he won't be there," Selma pointed out. "Well, he'll be there at night when he comes home, and who knows where that might lead?"

She broke into a laugh, and Elena could only shake her head. "You're both terrible friends," she said.

"Nah, you love us," Selma said.

"Actually, I wonder if that's what Jenna was thinking."

Elena turned toward Hannah with a frown. "What are you talking about?"

"Well, you know how she likes to play matchmaker. And she had to know that Brent would be coming home late. Maybe even wanting a drink before he goes to sleep. Oh, the possibilities…"

Elena frowned as she put an entire stick of butter into the skillet and turned the heat on low. "No way. Besides, why would she? You said I'm not that obvious, and Brent's not even interested."

Selma started humming under her breath as Elena diced the onion and peppers. "Maybe he is. If anyone would know, Jenna and Reece would. They're total besties."

Just the thought caused butterflies to do aerial acrobatics in Elena's stomach. "I'm going to burn the butter. Give it a rest, you two." She cast a stern look in both their directions, then used the edge of the knife to slide the onions and peppers into the hot, liquid butter. The mixture sizzled, and she breathed in the enticing aroma as she used a wooden spoon to stir the mix.

"What's going on with Easton and your parents?" she asked Hannah, mostly to change the subject. "And Selma, can you grate the cheese?"

Hannah scrunched up her nose as Selma moved around the bar. "They finally turned the money over to me."

"That's fantastic," Selma said, looking up from where she was rummaging in the fridge. "Matthew didn't tell me. The jerk. And, I'm sorry. I know they're your parents, but my brother is the nicest, most awesome guy in the world—except when he's being a jerk, and you and I are the only ones allowed to think that. And your parents are such total—"

"*Selma.*" Elena cut her friend off with a sharp word as she cracked the twelfth egg into a bowl, then gave the onions another quick stir.

Elena totally agreed that Hannah's mom and step-father had been vile in the way they'd treated her. Years ago, her birth father had died, earmarking a significant chunk of money for Hannah. But her mom remarried, and Hannah's stepfather later refused to give her the money. Elena didn't know the whole story, but she did know that it came to a head when Hannah fell in love with Matthew Herrington, a high school dropout who had made a success of himself by opening and running a series of popular gyms in the Austin area.

That kind of success wasn't good enough for Hannah's stepfather. Or, apparently, her mom.

"Easton threatened to sue," Hannah said, referring to Selma's fiancé and Hannah's law partner. "Of course, I have no case. My real dad named my mom as the beneficiary and only said he wanted it to go to me in some notes he left her. But since my stepfather is so concerned about his reputation in the business world, he caved. We agreed not to sue or talk to the media. He handed over the funds."

"And you and your mom?" Elena asked. She stirred the eggs, then signaled for Selma to bring over the cheese when she was done.

Hannah shrugged. "My family's here." She shot Selma a quick smile, then broadened it when she looked to Elena. "Matthew and you two and everybody at The Fix. And Shelby and my other friends from my old job." She lifted a shoulder in a half-shrug. "It's all good."

"And now you have the money for the law firm, right?" Elena asked. She remembered one night over drinks where Hannah had said that she wanted to use the money her dad left her to help finance the law firm that she and Easton recently opened.

"Still debating," Hannah said. "That was the original plan, but now the money just seems icky. I've got it in a money market until I decide. But that's definitely up there on the list. Of course, so are a vacation to Australia and some home renovations. So I guess we'll see."

"Well, it's a good problem to have." Elena hesitated, but then focused on adding the cheese to the eggs as she asked, "And you and your mom?"

"Yeah, right now I'd have to say that there is no me and my mom. But I'm okay with that. Not every problem gets solved and wrapped up with a silver bow. But I know that I have the money my dad wanted me to have. And that makes me happy."

"Good." Elena flashed what she hoped was a supportive smile. "It should." But even though she meant what she said, she couldn't shake the sense of shock and awe.

Because the truth was, Elena couldn't imagine defying her parents in the way that Hannah had. She was damn proud of her friend, true, but what if the dispute had been between her and Tyree?

She'd only just gotten to know her dad; could she close the door on their relationship like Hannah had with her mom?

She didn't know. And as she took the eggs off the heat, she damn sure hoped that she never had to find out.

Chapter Three

"RIGHT THERE," Brent said, tapping the pause button on his tablet's video player. "Do you see how he tilts his head up at the end? Right after he's finished spraying? The camera's not in the right place, but if I could enhance the video, I might be able to pull a few facial details."

Detective Landon Ware leaned forward, peering at the screen. "I doubt it."

Brent sighed, then sat back in the hard, plastic chair. Police departments tended not to splurge on furnishings, and the chairs in the break room were no exception. "Honestly, I doubt it, too," Brent said with a small shrug for his friend. "But I'm running out of options."

Landon nodded. "I get it. But man, you need to let it go."

In theory, Brent couldn't argue with that. In practice, he and Landon both knew he wasn't going to back down. They'd worked together before Brent had turned in his badge and taken up the mantle of head of security for The Fix on Sixth. They'd suffered through boring stakeouts and explosive raids. They'd shared beers and swapped life stories. And over the years, they'd become good friends. Which, of course, was why Brent had hauled himself to the police department's downtown station on a Saturday morning in September.

"It was probably just teens being assholes," Landon said, as if that would magically make Brent back off.

"Not teens." Brent thought of the vulgar graffiti that had covered almost the entire eastern exterior wall. "Not unless they were goaded on by adults."

"You sound certain."

"This wasn't the first incident."

Landon's brows rose with interest. "Yeah? Tyree hasn't mentioned a thing." The detective was engaged to Taylor D'Angelo, who worked as the stage manager for the Man of the Month contest. As a result, Landon had been spending even more time at the bar. Which meant he was hearing more of the gossip.

"I asked him not to. I don't want word spreading that he's disturbed by it. Or that he's investigating it."

"What's happened?"

"In addition to the tagging, a couple of broken window and some structural damage to a couple of the support columns. That one could have been bad if we hadn't caught it in time." As the head of security for The Fix, Brent's job ran the gamut from making sure all the employees had the proper ID and their references checked out, to investigating and pursuing any incidents against the property or its employees. And there'd been more incidents in the past month than he'd seen in all his years at The Fix. Whatever was going on, he was determined to find the perp and shut it down.

The corners of Landon's mouth curved into a frown. "What happened with the support?"

"Spencer noticed it."

"Was it part of the remodel they're doing for the show?" Brooke Hamlin and Spencer Dean were the stars of a real estate themed reality show that centered around a remodel of The Fix—with a little bit of sex appeal thrown in by virtue of the Man of the Month calendar guy contests that *The Business Plan* included in the show.

Brent shook his head. "The major structural work took place months ago, But Spencer's sharp. He saw the damage and realized it was vandalism. But the cameras were running, so that's not what he said. He told Tyree and me the full score later when the cameramen weren't around. And he offered to fix it for free."

"The broken windows … was that how the perp got in?"

"Found some denim threads on the glass. So it looks that way."

Landon studied him from across the interview table. "You have a theory."

"I think someone wants the property. And I think I know who."

"Make the place too much trouble, and figure Tyree

will sell to rid himself of an albatross? I get it. So who's doing it?"

"Well, I've narrowed the list down substantially. But if I want to make progress with any kind of speed, I need to figure out who's in that sweatshirt."

In truth, he was certain that the perp was someone from Bodacious, a competing bar, the owners of which had made no secret that they would be thrilled if Tyree disappeared so they could acquire The Fix's prime real estate.

"Fair enough. But like I said, there's no tech here that's gonna make that picture any clearer. I know it's been almost six years since you quit the force, but you know that as well as I do."

"I do," Brent admitted. "I was hoping you could pull some of the feed from the neighboring properties. And from that ATM across the street."

Landon exhaled slowly. "Come on, Brent. I need probable cause for that."

"Not if you have consent. Ask them. Remind them that the taggers could get their property next."

"Couldn't you do that?"

"I could. But I'm only security. You do it—even if you're asking for consent—and someone's going to think the cops are interested. And if I'm paying attention to folks' reactions to your poking around, I may realize who that is."

Landon shook his head, chuckling. "Fair enough. I'll have a few conversations. Meanwhile, why don't you get a few more cameras installed?"

Brent cocked his head as he looked at his friend. "Don't you think I've already put that in motion? They're coming late afternoon. Figured since I was going to be there anyway I may as well make some progress."

"Makes sense." Landon stood and started for the door, then paused, turning back to Brent. "I thought you were cutting down on weekend hours."

"I was. But I lost two of my guys recently. I'm covering shifts until I make some new hires. It's fine," he said, waving away whatever Landon had been about to say. "Sucks for Faith, but it's only temporary."

"Jenna covering babysitting duties for you?"

"Got someone else this time. I was going to ask her, but Reece mentioned in passing that they're in the middle of decorating the nursery. I didn't want to eat into her free time."

"Well, it sounds like you've got it under control. The kid stuff and the work stuff."

"It's what I do." He'd been juggling single parent-hood since Olivia had walked out on him the day that Faith was born. She'd been twenty-four when they'd married, and though he'd been a few years older, neither of them had truly understood what love was. From the moment she'd gotten pregnant, she'd pulled away from him. Hell, maybe that had started from the moment he'd slipped a ring on her finger.

Whatever had been brewing inside her had come to a head the night Faith was born. She snapped. She walked. And a few days later she filed for divorce, which had been fine with Brent. He could have forgiven a lot of things, but not walking out on their child.

"Have you thought about coming back?"

Brent's head snapped up, pulled from his thoughts by Landon's question. "I'm sorry. What?"

"To the job. We're short on detectives. You know the captain would give his right eye to have you back."

A frisson of excitement cut through him at the thought of going back on the job. But he pushed it down. "Not gonna happen," he said. "I believe you've met my daughter?"

Landon flashed a cockeyed grin. "And she's pretty damn adorable. But she's in kindergarten now. It's doable."

Brent nodded slowly. "It is. And honestly, it's tempting. I miss the job—I won't lie."

"Then what?"

"Come on, Landon. It's dangerous, and you know it. I'm not going to risk leaving her an orphan. She already had one parent leave. She's not going to lose another."

"Odds are slim, man."

"Maybe. But they're better now than if I were chasing down meth dealers. The only job that matters to me these days is being her dad."

Bottom line, as much as he missed being a cop, he was never going back.

He knew his priority, and her name was Faith.

Chapter Four

"DADDY!" Faith leaped off the swings and ran toward him, her little legs pumping and her black curls bouncing as Brent knelt on the grass in the well-manicured backyard.

"Hey, kiddo! Did you have fun? Sorry I'm late," he added to Rayleen Burg, the mother of Kyla, the birthday girl, who also happened to be Faith's current BFF. He didn't add that he'd gotten held up at the police station. The single mom was chatty enough as it was, and he didn't need to hand her conversational fodder. Especially since she'd made no attempt to hide her attraction to him.

Brent, however, didn't return the interest. True, she seemed like a nice woman. Smart. Personable. A good mom. But there were no sparks. More important, even if there were, he wasn't looking. He had no interest in getting attached to a woman. No interest in bringing a woman into Faith's life only to risk her walking right back out again.

"Kyla had a piñata! I got a kazoo and Starbursts. Can I have one when I get home?"

Starbursts were her favorite candy. "We'll see."

"They all had a great time," Rayleen said. "But I think someone might ask you about her own p-i-n-a-t-a for next Saturday."

"Is that so? Maybe you could email me the information where you bought yours?" Faith's sixth birthday party was in one week and by accepted neighborhood standards, he wasn't nearly prepared enough.

Rayleen laughed. "Happy to. And if you need any help getting ready, you just let me know." She pushed a lock of hair off her face and smiled prettily. "Kyla and Faith could play while we get ready."

"That's so generous of you," he said. "But I have some folks already lined up. Faith's aunt and uncle." Reece and Jenna might not actually be related, but they were definitely family. Of course, he hadn't yet enlisted their help, but he was confident they'd come if he called.

"Well, the offer stands." She flashed another smile, then waved acknowledgment when someone called to her from across the yard. "Either way, Kyla will be there. And thanks again for letting Faith come today."

"Of course," Brent said, as Faith descended, sliding down his body as if he were part of a jungle gym. He took her little hand in his, then let her tug him to the gate.

"Daddy! Where's the car?"

"Maybe I thought we'd walk home. But I can't remember how. Do you know the way?"

Her brow furrowed, and she put her hands on her hips. "Course, I do, Daddy. But you didn't really forget, did you? You wouldn't forget how to come home, would you?"

Brent's heart twisted. He doubted that Faith was thinking of Olivia—she sometimes talked about getting a mom, but there was never any mention of the mom who had left. But even so, it was Olivia who was on his mind now.

"I'd never forget how to come home to you, munchkin. I'm just pretending."

The smile returned in full force. "I knew you were."

"That's because you're so smart."

"I counted all the way to two hundred today. Bobby Carmichael bet that I couldn't, but I did. And he had to give me his gummy bears."

Brent arched a brow. "I thought you only had Starbursts."

"I gave the gummy bears away. But I still won them."

"Well, congratulations."

"Look both ways, Daddy."

They'd reached the four-way stop sign two blocks from their house. Brent did as Faith ordered, then asked, "Now what?"

"Now you can go, but only with a grown-up."

"And?"

"And pay attention."

"Good girl. Come on."

They started walking, Faith's head swiveling as they crossed from one side to the other. "Can we go to the zoo today, Daddy?"

That heavy feeling returned to his gut. "I wish I could, but I have to go to work today, and there's not time."

"Oh." He hated that tone of disappointment.

"You know I have a job, sweetie. And sometimes I have to work weekends."

"Can I come? Patrick's daddy takes him to work on Saturdays. Patrick colors in the conference room. His daddy's a lawyer. He told me so."

"Unfortunately, your daddy doesn't have a conference room. And where I work isn't a good place for little girls. But I have someone super special coming to watch you later."

"Jenna?"

"Aunt Jenna and Uncle Reece already have plans. But Miss Elena is coming. Does that sound good?"

"She pulled me in the wagon when we were at Uncle Tyree's, and Eli told me she used to live by the beach."

"She did. In California."

"I've never seen a beach."

"Someday, kiddo." Right now, he was just happy that Elena's beach credentials apparently increased her appeal as a babysitter. "So you guys will have fun, right?"

Faith's head bobbed affirmatively, and for the millionth time, Brent wondered how he'd gotten so lucky to have such an amazing daughter. "She's funny." Faith smiled up at him. "And she's pretty, too. Do you think she's pretty, Daddy?"

His mouth went dry, his body kicking into that same state of hyperawareness he felt every time he was near her. "Very pretty," he said, and hoped his voice sounded normal.

"She's nice, too. I like her, Daddy," she said with a firm nod of her little head. "It's okay if you have her babysit me anytime."

He managed to keep a straight face. "Well, thank you for the permission. I'm happy you approve."

"Do you like her, too?"

He glanced down, looking into her earnest little face. Did she mean like? Or *like*?

Either way, the answer was yes. Although the answer to the second intonation was one he should keep to himself. "Yes, I do," he said. "I'd never let someone I didn't like watch my bestest girl. Would I?"

For a minute or two, they walked in silence. They were three houses away from home when she asked, "Do you like her the way Uncle Reece likes Aunt Jenna?"

For a second, Brent's heart stopped, and he quickly assured his daughter that Elena was only a friend.

But at the same time, he wondered how much Faith had seen. She'd only been around him and Elena a couple of times. Was she asking because she was five and kids asked all sorts of embarrassing questions? Or was she asking because she'd picked up on his vibes, and kids noticed all sorts of things you wish they wouldn't?

And if it was the latter, was she the only one who'd noticed his growing attraction to Elena? Or had his friends picked up on it, too? Jenna, maybe. She noticed everything related to her friends' love lives. But she hadn't said a word, so maybe he was in the clear.

Reece? Doubtful. Like himself, Reece was generally clueless about things like that. Tyree? Brent hoped his friend hadn't noticed. Almost as much as he hoped Elena herself had no clue. Because no matter how much he might be attracted to that stunning, fascinating woman, it wasn't going anywhere. And he was absolutely not having a sex-only fling with his good friend's daughter.

Not that he wasn't tempted. And not that he'd been a monk since Olivia left. With Faith, of course, there wasn't much time for women, especially since he was damn sure not bringing a one-night stand back to the house. But there'd been a handful of times when he'd met a woman at the bar—usually a tourist so that he knew she wouldn't stay—and they'd hit it off enough to end up back in her hotel room.

Jenna was convinced that he was miserable and would shrivel up if he didn't get out and start dating, so he let her believe that not only was there some real interest with those sporadic women, but also that he saw more women than he really did. The truth was that he only hooked up when he was having a bad day, craving not only adult companionship, but physical release. Usually, though, he took care of that himself. He didn't like using women that way, and he didn't like the hollow feeling that inevitably settled over him once it was over.

Better to just be Faith's dad right now. Maybe someday he'd try for a relationship, but not until Faith was older. And definitely not until he was one hundred percent sure that any woman he brought into their life was in for the long haul.

"Daddy?" She tugged at his hand, and he looked down, startled out of his thoughts.

"Sorry, kiddo. Mind wandering."

"Can we watch a movie before you go?"

He did some mental calculations and started to say no. He needed to sit at his desk and pay some bills, and if they watched a movie, he'd have less than ten minutes to get changed and out the door once it ended.

"Of course, we can," he said. Screw the bills. He'd

pay them when he got home. Easy to work at three in the morning, anyway. God knows he'd have peace and quiet. "How about *Finding Nemo*? That's almost like going to a beach."

She clapped her hands gleefully, then ran up the sidewalk to their front door, where she switched from clapping to bouncing. "Popcorn, too? With lots and lots of butter?"

"You got it." He'd have to tell Elena to be sure and get some real food into his kiddo that evening. But right now, buttery popcorn on a Saturday with his best girl and a cartoon fish sounded like a damn good time.

Chapter Five
_____

ELENA PULLED down the visor on her tiny Honda and checked her makeup. Frowning, she reached for her purse—her lipstick was slightly smeared—then yanked her hand back as if she'd been bitten by a snake.

What on earth was she doing? Here she was, parked in front of Brent's house so that she could go babysit —*babysit*—and she was checking her freaking makeup? Clearly she had lost her mind.

Faith couldn't care less if her Cranberry Wine was smudged. And as for Brent ... well, she was certain he didn't care either. And she shouldn't care. In fact...

She let the thought trail off as she bent over, then

retrieved the box of tissues from the passenger seat floorboard. She tugged out a tissue, wiped it violently over her mouth, then checked herself in the mirror again. Mostly gone. Just a hint of the plum-rose tint that flattered her dark skin. Good. She still looked put together, but not like she'd been trying too hard.

Good Lord. Was she really wasting time thinking about this? Brent wasn't going to notice one way or another. And she needed to just push the man right out of her head.

Easier said than done, though. She hadn't had an actual, solid infatuation since Raymond Jackson in eleventh grade. She was a grown woman; fantasies were one thing—and yes, she fantasized about Brent far too often. But actual crushes were absurd.

And yet here she was, completely pre-occupied with the man. And apparently also completely unable to banish him from her thoughts.

She should have said no. She should have sucked it up, shaken her head, and told Jenna and Brent and the whole wide world that she absolutely couldn't babysit.

But she hadn't. And she couldn't let him down now.

She drew in a cleansing breath, exhaled, then stepped out of the car. She'd been to Brent's bungalow in Austin's Crestview neighborhood before, but today she paid more attention as she walked slowly up the sidewalk to the front door. The lawn was perfectly trimmed, the patio surrounded by flowering shrubs. The front door had been recently painted a deep blue, and the wooden porch gleamed a sparkling white.

Brent was a man who knew how to take care of things, something she would have guessed from the way he took care of The Fix and his daughter, but it was nice to see it played out in other aspects of his life.

Then again, maybe she was just being overly analytical to buy time.

Not that she had a reason in the world to be nervous. This wasn't a date. She'd come to babysit. He wasn't interested in anything more. And that, she told herself firmly, was for the best.

Before she could launch into another bout of nerves, she rang the doorbell, then smiled at the pounding of little feet. A second later, the door flew open and Faith stood there, her eyes wide and her cheeks red with exertion.

"Elena! We just watched Nemo!"

"That's great. I love Dory, especially. And the seagulls."

"Mine!" the little girl said, in a near-perfect imitation of the gulls from the movie. She stepped back, giving Elena room to enter. "We're going to have fun. Daddy said so."

"Then I guess it must be true." She smiled at Brent who stepped in from the kitchen, a dish towel in his hands.

"Sorry. Someone had a little popcorn with her butter. I needed to wash off the greasiness."

Faith looked at her hands, grimaced, then wiped them on her jeans.

"You. Go wash."

"Okay, Daddy." She started to trot that way, but he held out a hand, stopping her.

"Did you ask who it was before you pulled open the door?"

"But it was Elena! We *like* her!" Her voice rose with indignation, and Elena bit back a smile, pleased to be among the welcome elite.

"We do," Brent said, aiming a wink at Elena that made her insides go all gooey. "But unless you have X-ray vision that I don't know about, you didn't know for sure it was Elena until after you opened the door. *Do* you have X-ray vision?"

She shook her head. "No, Daddy."

"What's the rule?"

"Always ask who it is before opening the door."

"And?"

Little shoulders rose and fell with a five-year-old's version of guilt-plus-exasperation. "And if I don't know who it is, then I'm not allowed to open the door. But I *do* know Elena. So I shouldn't be in trouble."

"Mmmm. Not how it works, kiddo. Go on." He gave her a light pat on the bottom. "Wash your hands, then come back in here."

"Okay." She started toward her room, then paused to look back at Elena. "I'm glad you're here. And you really are pretty. Daddy said so." Then she turned and scampered down the hallway, leaving Elena to tame the wild butterflies that had begun dancing in her belly.

Brent shot her a quick glance before shaking his head in exasperation as he watched his daughter disappear.

"Did you really say that?" She knew she shouldn't ask, but somehow she couldn't keep her mouth shut any more than she could turn off the pleasant tingles that were spreading through her body.

He cleared his throat as he stuck his hands in his pockets. "I did," he said, lifting his head to meet her eyes. "Although I was saying it in agreement with Faith's assessment. A little fact she conveniently left out."

She took a further step into the living room, emboldened by his admission. "So you're not just running around telling the world you think I'm pretty?"

"No."

"But you do think so?"

"I just said I did."

She swallowed, knowing she should be quiet, but unable to still her tongue. "I'm glad to hear it," she said, then added in a whisper, "It matters to me what you think."

His head tilted almost imperceptibly, but she'd paid enough attention to him over the last few months to recognize his subtle signals. He was interested. And a little bit unsure. "And why's that?" he finally said.

Her throat tightened, and she wondered if he could hear the pounding of her heart. She almost lost her nerve, but this was opportunity knocking loud and hard, and she'd be a fool to ignore it. "Don't you know?"

He didn't answer. Instead, he simply held her gaze as she kicked herself. She should have said nothing. Or she should have said more. Instead, she'd played it coy, and what if he didn't know? What if he didn't understand at all?

"Elena."

That was all he said, but she thought she heard longing in his voice. Or was that just her imagination? She didn't know. All she knew was that he was looking right at her, and she was starting to feel a little drunk as she stared into those whiskey colored eyes.

A moment passed, then another. And finally she found her voice. "Yes?"

His throat moved as he swallowed. "I think I should show you the kitchen. I've got some leftovers Faith can have for dinner."

"Oh." She felt as if she'd fallen out of a cozy boat into a freezing ocean. "Right."

"I'll be home late. Probably three. You're up for this?"

"Of course." She conjured a smile before following him to the kitchen. "I'm up for whatever you need."

Unfortunately, she could tell perfectly well that he didn't need her.

Chapter Six

BRENT HAD a hell of a time keeping his mind on work. Instead, he kept thinking of Elena. Of her sweet smile. Her lithe body.

Of her seemingly innocent words that weren't innocent at all.

Whatever you need.

God, did she even know what she was offering? Because he wanted a lot. Too bad he couldn't take what she was offering.

What he *thought* she was offering.

But no. He wasn't that dense. She was interested. And God knew he was interested.

But that didn't mean it was a good idea. On the contrary, he thought, glancing over at where Tyree stood with Reece at the other end of the long oak bar, it was about as bad as an idea could get.

"You look distracted," Jenna said, keeping her hand on her belly as she hauled herself up and onto one of the nearby barstools.

"I'm not distracted," he protested. "What makes you say I'm distracted?"

She laughed. "Maybe the way you've been staring at that proposal for the last ten minutes."

He glanced down at the folder he held open in his hands and the sheath of papers that comprised the security company's plan for installing an upgraded camera system.

"Sorry. I was just—"

"Thinking about camera placement?" she interrupted, her tone innocent. "Why wouldn't you be? After all, cameras are fascinating, and you need to spend lots and lots of time second-guessing the experts you hired to analyze the visual gaps and do the installation."

He put the folder down and stared at this woman

who was one of his two best friends. "All right. I give up. What's up with you?"

"Not a thing," she said, then smiled sweetly. "So how were Elena and Faith getting along when you left?"

"Gangbusters," he said, his eyes narrowing as he took in her too-innocent expression. "It's not a good idea, Jenna."

To her credit, she didn't pretend to misunderstand. Instead, she just said, "Isn't it?"

He sighed. This wasn't a conversation he wanted to have, but he knew Jenna's matchmaking tendencies well enough to know that there was no way out now. "She's too young."

"Oh, please." Jenna sipped the water that Cam, the weekend manager, put in front of her, then turned her attention back to Brent. "If she was thirty-three and you were forty-three, you wouldn't even give a flip."

"Probably true," he conceded. "But by thirty-three she'd have a sense of her life. Some stability in her career. At twenty-three, she's barely starting out. She's in grad school. You know that right?"

"And, what? At thirty you magically cross some line that makes you established and stable? If that's the case, why haven't you settled down with a thirty-something already? God knows enough women who qualify have passed through these doors and left you their number. And don't deny it, because I've seen the napkins you've thrown out. Lots of heartbroken women out there, Brent."

"Don't push me, Jenna."

For a second, she looked like she was going to argue. Then she sighed and laced her fingers over her growing belly. "Look, I get it. I really do. But not all women leave, you know? And I want you to be happy."

"Who says I'm not?" And he was happy. He had his friends. He had Faith. He had work he enjoyed even if it didn't have the rush of his previous life as a detective. Bottom line, he was genuinely a happy man. But that didn't mean there wasn't something missing.

That part, however, he didn't say to Jenna.

She understood it anyway, of course. "Take a chance, Brent. Just one tiny step outside of your circle. You owe it to yourself."

"No, I don't. The only one I owe anything to is Faith. It's just her and me against the world. You know that. And with her, I'm not willing to take chances."

Jenna's shoulders sank on a sigh. She knew his history. Knew that his mother had passed away his first year of college from ovarian cancer. Her death had driven a wedge between Brent and his father because his dad had pulled away from Brent, going so far as to move to Oregon. Brent had given the man his space, figuring they'd be able to mend the rift after his dad had healed. But then his father was killed in a fatal one-car accident, and even now, Brent didn't know if it was truly accidental or if it had been vehicular suicide.

Either way, he knew better than most that people left. And even though he couldn't shield Faith from death, he could damn sure reduce the risk that the people she loved would walk out of her life.

"You have us," Jenna said softly. "And so does Faith. You know that, Brent. And not every woman is Olivia. I mean, I'm not leaving Reece. He's stuck with me." She flashed a bright grin, her green eyes flashing. "I thought I should mention that. Just in case you were worried."

"Thanks for that," he said, amused despite himself. "Now go away," he added, picking up the folder again. "I really do have to read this and get back to these guys about the installation details."

"Fair enough."

He helped her get off the chair, then smiled as she made the sign of a B on her forehead. "Best friends forever?"

"You know it," he said, making the sign right back.

She rose on her toes to kiss his cheek, then headed back to handle her own work as he tried to focus on the camera installation proposal.

For the most part, he managed to get the day's work done. But her words clung to him as he signed the proposal and emailed it back, and as he called Landon to go over everything the detective had learned when he'd canvassed the neighborhood. On the whole, all of his attention that Saturday was focused on preventing further graffiti and finding the original taggers.

And yet there was Elena, too, a constant presence beneath his thoughts. A sensual awareness that he couldn't shake, and that he told himself he didn't want.

But he did.

Damn him, he really did.

She was still on his mind when he finally made it home at half-past three in the morning. The house was dark except for the flicker of the muted television and the bathroom light in the hall, kept on always at Faith's insistence.

He saw Elena on the couch and started to speak, then realized that she was asleep. Gingerly, he tiptoed past, then walked quietly to Faith's room to check on the little girl who was snoring softly and cuddling Cracker Jack, a stuffed lemur that had become her newest lovey.

He bent to kiss her cheek, then gently closed her door, leaving only a crack, before heading back to the living room. "Hey," he said, bending over and placing a light hand on Elena's shoulder.

He shook her gently. "Time to go," he whispered, then sucked in a surprised breath when she shifted in her sleep and reached for his hand. She made the kind of soft noise that made a man hard, then drew their joined hands to her lips before gently pressing a kiss to his knuckles.

Electricity arced through him, but he stood frozen, afraid that if he even breathed he'd lose it. But oh, how he wanted to move. Wanted to touch her. Wanted to wake her, then kiss her.

Wanted to do all sorts of things he shouldn't want to do at all. And yet he did want to. He wanted to desperately.

Finally, he stepped back, gently tugging his hand free. He didn't try to wake her again. Instead, he told himself that she was fast asleep. But it wasn't a convincing lie; he knew damn well that the only reason he didn't send her home was that he liked having her in his house.

He pulled an extra blanket from the basket by the television, then draped it over her. Then he went to his own bed and tried to sleep.

Instead, he tossed and turned, though at some point sleep must have caught up with him, because he was startled awake when his alarm went off at eight.

With more alacrity than usual for a Sunday morning, he sprang out of bed, then grabbed his robe before heading into the living room. He expected to see her, of course, and when he saw that the living room was empty, he couldn't shake the hollow feeling, as if he'd suffered a profound loss.

He told himself it was just the shock of a change of plans—he'd intended to make waffles for her and Faith—but of course that wasn't it at all. He'd wanted to see her. More than that, he'd wanted Elena to be the first person he saw that morning, even before seeing Faith.

"Not good, Sinclair. Really not good."

"What's not good, Daddy?"

He painted on a smile as he turned to his daughter. "Hey you, sneaking up on me. How was it last night with Elena?"

"She made me spaghetti, and we baked cookies and played games," she said. "And I won all the hide-and-seek!"

"I bet you did." He listened to her chatter on about where she hid and the silly songs they sang and the intricate process of making perfect slice-and-bake cookies. Then he plunked her on the counter while he made them both waffles before sending her out to the front yard to retrieve the Sunday paper. They settled down on the sofa, and he read the news while she looked at the funnies and the ad inserts. After that, they went to the grocery store, and he supervised the cleaning of her room.

All in all, a typical Sunday, until the doorbell rang at one, announcing Elena's return.

"Elena!" Faith called when Brent opened the door for her.

"Hey, kiddo." Elena knelt, then wrapped her arms around the wriggling little girl. She held tight to Faith as she looked up at Brent. "You should have woken me. I didn't mean to camp out in your living room. Sorry."

"No worries. You looked so peaceful that I didn't want to disturb you." Not exactly the truth, but it would do.

"I had the strangest dream," she said, making his stomach tighten. Surely she hadn't really been awake.

"Yeah? What was it?"

She shook her head. "I can't remember. Just that it

was strange. But nice." She flashed that wide, beautiful smile, and he felt himself go weak in the knees. He really did have it bad. *Damn.*

"I was sorry you were gone when I woke up," he said, though the words had escaped of their own accord, and he immediately wished he could call them back.

"Yeah?" She didn't look freaked out by the strange admission. Instead, she looked pleased.

"I make a waffle to rival your dad's. I'd planned to make one for you, too."

Her whole face seemed to glow. "That's so sweet. Any morning you want to make one for me, just say so."

He swallowed, trying to clear his head. But everything with this woman seemed to have a double meaning, and he was undoubtedly going to dig himself a very deep hole.

"Right. Well, I need to run. Thanks for coming early today. I'm trying to follow up some leads about those taggers." Specifically, he was going to go over the security footage that Landon had managed to get from the other nearby establishments.

Her brow furrowed. "Aren't the police handling it?"

"They are. But I'm doing what I can. I used to be one of the police, remember?"

"A detective. I know. More's the pity."

He peered at her, confused. "What?"

"Detectives don't wear uniforms." Her voice had gone deeper, and just a little husky. "And I bet you looked great in a uniform."

He took a single step toward her. "What are you doing, Elena?"

She glanced down, but when she looked up again, he saw strength in those chocolate brown eyes. "Just being honest. You said I was pretty, remember? I think we're even now."

He said nothing.

"Do you miss it?"

He shook his head, confused.

"Being a detective," she clarified.

He waited a beat before answering, then nodded. "Yeah. I do. But it's a hazardous job. I have more important responsibilities."

"Yes, you do. And you don't take many risks, do you, Brent?"

He looked her straight in the eye, his heart pounding in protest of his words. "No, Elena. I really don't."

Chapter Seven

"THANKS FOR HELPING ME WITH THIS," Elena said to her dad as she checked the temperature of the two round yellow cakes she'd pulled from the oven in Tyree's kitchen an hour ago.

"Cool enough to frost?" he asked.

"Yup," she said. Faith had told her and Brent that she wanted a homemade cake for her party tomorrow, and when Brent told Elena that he'd yet to make a cake that wasn't lopsided and dry, she'd volunteered. Then she'd roped in her dad.

"You don't have to thank me. We've been cooking together enough these past few months, so you should know I'm happy to do it. For you and for Faith."

"Not for Brent?" As soon as she asked the question, she regretted it. She'd been on pins and needles around Tyree for almost a week now, ever since she started babysitting for Brent.

For that matter, she'd been cool and distant around Brent, too, her own demeanor matching his. The electricity still crackled between them, but ever since he'd shut down their flirtation on Sunday, he'd been coolly polite. To her face, anyway.

Every once in a while she'd catch him looking at her in a way that set her body humming. But those moments lasted only seconds, and only when he thought she wasn't paying attention. And two nights ago she'd awakened when he'd come into the house at a quarter to four. She'd pretended to be asleep, though, and when he sat on the coffee table just inches from where she lay on the couch, she'd been terrified that the wild pounding of her heart would give her away.

After a few moments, he'd rested his hand on her bare shoulder where the sleeve of her oversized T-shirt had slipped off. His touch had lingered for a few seconds longer than necessary before he'd gently shaken her as he whispered her name. She'd pretended to rouse groggily from a deep sleep, but at the time, she'd never felt so awake, and even now she could recall the sensation of his hand against her bare skin.

She wanted more, and she felt her cheeks heat as she quickly concentrated on measuring the confectioner's sugar.

Beside her, Tyree hesitated before he measured out the cocoa and poured it into the mixing bowl. Just a minor hitch, and she would have missed it if she hadn't been looking. But she had been.

"Daddy?"

He turned to her, a tight smile on his kind face.

"What is it?" she pressed.

He sighed, then reached for the butter. "We need to cream these together."

"You know that's not what I meant. What about doing it for Brent?"

"You really want to have this conversation?" His voice was level, but she could hear the frustration underneath.

No, she really didn't.

"Yes," she said firmly. "I do."

He exhaled. "Fine. What's going on with you two?"

"Nothing." She spat the word out, unprepared for him to actually dive straight to the heart of the matter.

His brows rose and she took an involuntary step back.

"Honest," she said, crossing her heart. "There's nothing going on."

"Good," Tyree said. "Keep it that way."

She frowned. As far as she could tell, she had no choice in that regard. She'd been babysitting Faith now for one entire week, and although the tension between her and Brent kept getting thicker and thicker, he hadn't made a single move. And, of course, neither had she.

Maybe it was just her imagination.

It couldn't be her imagination.

Could it?

"Elena?"

She turned to see him regarding her, his expression unreadable. He said nothing, and neither did she. A standoff, apparently. And she was the one who lost, because ultimately she just couldn't take it anymore. "What's wrong with him? I mean, I thought he was your friend."

"And I thought there was nothing between you."

"You got that right. He has zero interest in having anything to do with me."

He hesitated before beating in the sugar and milk. "You, however, are hovering somewhere above zero?"

She didn't answer. Just looked at him defiantly until his shoulders moved, as if he was shifting a weighty burden.

"Brent's a good friend and one of the best men I know. Smart and loyal and kind."

"Then what?"

"Ah, *mon bijou*. He's almost ten years older than you."

"So? You and Mom were young."

"Don't pretend to be naive, Elena. I haven't known you long, but I know you well. And I know that you have aspirations. Dreams. And those dreams don't involve staying in Austin."

"I—" She wanted to protest, but he was right. Ultimately, she wanted to work for a consulting company that would send her around the country, visiting small towns with historic roots so that she could help plan their growth.

"I'm not going to tell you who to see, but I will say that Brent's not just a man. He's a father. And he knows it would be all too easy to hurt that little girl."

"Daddy, I—"

"You should add that sugar now," he said, and she knew the conversation was over.

She thought of Hannah and her parents and the tension between them now because of Matthew. She didn't want that with Tyree, not when they'd just discovered each other.

But she didn't want to ignore whatever this thing was between her and Brent, either.

At the moment, it really didn't matter, as the only interesting stuff with Brent was happening inside her head. But what if someday those tight wires keeping them apart snapped, and she found herself in his arms? Tyree was right, after all. She'd be gone in a few years. And Brent would never do anything that might hurt Faith.

Which meant that they were over before they'd begun, and all she had to cling to were fantasies.

SIX YEARS.

How the hell had six years already flown by?

Brent sat on the stone bench under the pecan tree and watched as the princesses and pirates chased each other around the backyard, their squeals probably carrying all the way back to The Fix downtown.

"I think the theme was a hit," Elena said, stepping up beside him. "Good job."

He laughed. "You're the one who suggested it—and thank you for that—all I did was get online and order everything princess and pirate related that would get here in time. Fortunately, that was a lot."

The pink and black covered card tables were awash in paraphernalia. Plastic scepters and cutlasses. Tiaras and eye patches. Even dresses for the princesses and hats for the pirates.

"And all the kids are having a blast. Especially Faith. And that's what matters."

"Yes, it is," he agreed. Faith, with a combination of Birthday Girl resolve and strong will, had decided that she was a Pirate Princess. She wore a pink dress, carried a cutlass, and had a tiara lodged onto the black pirate hat.

He tilted his head up to look at Elena, then slid over to make room on the bench. She sat, but he hadn't calculated just how small the bench was for two adults. Usually he shared this space with Faith.

The air between them seemed thick with possibilities, and he forced each and every one from his mind. "I was just thinking that it's been six years. Time flies."

"It definitely does."

"You'll be out of grad school in no time."

She laughed. "True. But considering I just got started, don't get rid of me so soon."

He'd been thinking the opposite, already regretting the moment she would inevitably leave. But before he could tell her that, Rayleen approached.

"Such a lovely party," she said. "I'm sorry I need to take Kyla away early. It's her dad's weekend."

"Of course," he said, his heart twisting at the thought of only having Faith part of the time. "Faith," he called, but she was too busy running her kingdom to hear.

"I'll go get her," Elena said. "I'll send her over to you and Kyla," she added to Rayleen before diving into the throng.

As Rayleen headed back toward the gate, Brent watched Elena navigate the horde of kids, and he had to admit she did a great job. She was a natural with them, and Faith adored her. She'd also made the cake and conceived the theme. Basically, she'd slid into the role of hostess without him even realizing.

He waited for a wave of irritation to hit him. A reaction to the simple fact that she'd infiltrated herself into their family routine. But the irritation didn't come. The truth was, he appreciated the help.

He told himself it was no different than when Jenna helped. That, of course, was a lie for a lot of reasons, not the least of which was that he didn't want to sleep with Jenna. And he did want that with Elena. More and more each day, actually, despite his best efforts to shut his libido down.

Now he stood, planning to go inside for some of the beer and barbecue that Elena had suggested he provide for the adults. He didn't make it that far, though, as Reece sidled up beside him, then handed him a Sam Adams lager. "I was just coming to get one of these."

"Guess I read your mind. What are friends for?"

They clinked the bottles, then both took long draws. Brent noticed that Reece looked in Elena's direction, but he said nothing about her. Instead, he nodded toward Landon and Taylor.

"They make a good couple," Reece said.

"They do," Brent agreed, but there was a wariness in his tone. He knew the parallels to him and Elena as well as Reece did. An interracial romance. A younger woman.

And he wasn't at all surprised when Reece said, "Your dad would never have approved of them."

He turned to his friend, knowing full well that Reece was really talking about him and Elena. "No," he said. "He wouldn't. But I never agreed with the old man much anyway."

"True that, and I'm glad to hear it. Would be a shame to let a stupid prejudice get in the way of something that could be good." He turned to face Brent. "More to the point, it would be a shame if a stupid fear got in the way, too."

"You've been talking to Jenna," Brent said.

Reece lifted a shoulder, the tattooed sleeves on his arm seeming to dance with the motion. "Well, she's my wife. We talk sometimes." They'd been married in a small ceremony a few weeks ago with a justice of the peace, and they'd kept that news mostly to themselves, intending to have a bigger ceremony with a reception after the baby was born.

"Landon doesn't have a kid," Brent said. "If Taylor pulls an Olivia, the only one she's hurting is him."

Reece nodded slowly. "That's true. But how long are you going to hide behind what ifs?"

And then, before Brent could respond, Reece stepped away and slipped among the children, leaving Brent behind, still tasting those words.

Chapter Eight

THE WEEK BEFORE, Brent had hired one new guy for his security team. And although he couldn't fully shift back to a managerial role until he had both new men in place, the addition of Owen meant that he could at least go home early on a few nights.

And Sunday, thank goodness, was one of them.

He'd told Elena, of course. And although he would miss seeing her asleep on the couch when he arrived home after three, he couldn't deny the anticipation he felt at knowing she'd be awake when he walked in the door.

What he hadn't expected was to find her in the kitchen surrounded by an explosion of flour, and his little girl wide-awake and bouncing gleefully on her countertop perch.

"Daddy!" Faith shrieked.

"I am so sorry," Elena said at the same time, wiping her nose and leaving a white streak across her skin. "Faith forgot to mention that her class is having a party for her birthday on Monday, so I'm making her cupcakes to take. And when I mentioned that my birthday is tomorrow, she insisted on helping with the cupcakes so that I could take one home as a birthday treat."

"Happy birthday," he said, amused. "I assume that Hurricane Faith was the cause of all this." He indicated the room.

"We had planned to get it all clean before you got home, didn't we?"

Faith nodded. "We made a mess."

"And it's past your bedtime." She looked up at Brent. "I'll still clean it. Just let me get her to bed first."

"It's really okay."

"No." She sounded both flustered and determined. "I've got it. You just, um, have some coffee." She poured him a cup and shoved it toward him. "Enjoy."

"Right. Got it. Will do." He felt his lips twitch with amusement, and looked down before she noticed. "Give me a hug," he said, then set his coffee down so he could catch the little girl who threw herself into his arms. He squeezed her tight, then kissed her forehead. "Night, sweetie. Go with Miss Elena."

"Okay, Daddy," she said, then disappeared down the hall with her flour-smudged babysitter.

The coffee was fine, but he thought the evening called for wine, and he grabbed a bottle from the small wine fridge he had tucked in the corner. A nice red, which he poured for both himself and Elena. He was halfway through his glass when she returned.

"I think she's finally asleep," Elena said. "About all of this——"

"It's nothing," he said, interrupting what was sure to be another apology. "Here. We'll toast your birthday."

She grinned. "Yeah?"

He'd never seen her look frazzled before. Now her short hair was mussed and her makeup smudged. He'd thought she was beautiful before, but now she looked vulnerable, too. And he wasn't sure that was a good thing.

"I'm really sorry she wasn't asleep when you got home," she added. "I know how late it is. But she wanted to watch another cartoon, and we picked *The Incredibles*, and I think it just got her all worked up. I had no idea she'd get out of bed to start building a fort for her stuffed animals while I was making the cupcakes. And then when we were taking it apart, I mentioned about my birthday tomorrow, and that's when all hell broke loose in the kitchen."

She glanced around the room, frowning. "I think there are one or two spots where we managed to not get any flour."

"No worries," he said with a small chuckle. "Truly. That kid has a talent for making messes. And I assure you I'm prepared for massive crankiness tomorrow."

He saw her horrified look and wished he'd stayed silent. He didn't like seeing Elena Anderson upset. And every time he'd seen her that way, he'd had to fight the urge to pull her into his arms and kiss the worry right off her face.

And that definitely wasn't the direction his mind needed to be going. Not with her. Not with his boss and friend's daughter. And definitely not with his babysitter.

No matter how tempted he might be.

"Seriously," he said to reassure her, "it's no big deal. Kids stay up late. They sneak out of bed. It happens. And I really appreciate you helping me out like this. I know childcare wasn't what you had in mind when you started graduate school."

"Well, in case you forgot, you're paying me."

He laughed. "Good point. Even so. There are times when there's not enough pay in the world." He glanced around the kitchen. "I'm thinking today is one of those days."

"It's definitely up there," she admitted. "But really, I'm happy to help. She's a great kid, and the job works with my schedule. You know how grad school is."

"I don't actually. Cop. Security specialist. Now bar owner and partner to your father," he added, because he really needed to say that out loud. A reminder to them both. Because even though he'd been telling himself for months that it was his imagination, he knew damn well that Elena was attracted to him, too.

He kept trying to push it from his mind, but the truth was that lightning had positively crackled between them the first time they'd met. And more than once he'd caught her looking at him, the desire so palpable that he'd had to turn away and imagine cold showers and other non-sensual things.

He was a wreck, and it was no good telling himself that because it had been so long since he'd had a woman in his bed, he was starved for any woman.

She flashed a sweet, almost shy smile, and his stomach flip-flopped.

No. This was all about Elena. Only Elena.

"This is nice," she said. "Chatting, I mean. Usually

I'm either comatose when you get back or else I rush out the door so I can get home and crash."

"Well, I can't let you risk ruining the cupcakes."

"That's something else I'm sorry for. I should have called to clear it with you. So I hope you don't mind."

"I don't mind at all. I just…"

"Yes?"

How could he say that the room seemed too small, but he knew damn well that it wasn't because of the heat from the oven?

"Nothing," he said instead. "Forgot what I was going to say."

She cocked her head, a question in her eyes, and for a second he thought she might be about to call him out on his lie. He almost hoped she would.

Bing!

"Done," she said, her voice a little too bright, as if that would combat the tension in the room.

She bent to take them out, and Brent forced himself

not to study the perfect curve of her ass in her Lucky jeans.

Lucky. Wasn't that ironic?

She put the cupcake pans on trivets, then took off the oven mitts. "Well. There. I guess I should get going."

"Don't they need to cool?"

She nodded. "I figure you've done this before, right? Faith can frost them in the morning. I didn't make fresh, but I saw you have a couple of cans of frosting in the pantry."

"It's one of the major food groups," he said.

She rolled her eyes. "So you frost them, then put them in some Tupperware."

"Right. I could do that. Or you could stay and make sure I don't put them away too soon."

She swallowed. "Well, yeah. If that would help you out."

He took one step toward her, and in the small kitchen that put them only inches apart. "Or you could forget about the cupcakes and just stay."

"I—Brent." She licked her lips, and his whole body tightened with desire. "What are you doing?"

"Honestly? I'm thinking about kissing you."

"Oh." He saw both surprise and pleasure in her eyes. "What about it?"

"How much I want to. How much I shouldn't."

"Why not?" The question was breathy, almost a whisper.

"For one, you're younger than me. You're my boss's daughter. My friend's daughter. Not to mention that I'm a single dad who needs to be careful about the signals I send to my kid. Plus, you're the babysitter."

"Those are all bad?"

He sighed. "I thought so. I'm starting to lose perspective."

"I can help with that."

"Can you?"

"Yeah." She took a step toward him, then rose up on her tiptoes. Gently, she brushed a kiss over his lips.

Then she backed away, biting her lower lip as she looked at him, as if challenging him to do more.

Dammit, he took the challenge. Maybe he'd go straight to hell, but he had to have this woman. And without any more hesitation, he pulled her close, then claimed her mouth in a kiss that seared through him, long and hot and deep.

Chapter Nine

ELENA MELTED AGAINST HIM, shocked that she'd been so bold as to take the initiative and wildly happy that he'd stepped up to the plate once she had. This kiss was … well, it was everything. For months, she'd been imagining his lips on hers, his tongue warring with hers, his hands touching her everywhere. And now—oh, dear Lord, he was doing to her exactly what she'd imagined. Touching. Tasting. Teasing.

Taking.

"Christ, Elena, you taste like ambrosia." He broke their kiss only long enough to murmur those sensual words, and then his mouth closed over hers again. It was already hot in the kitchen, but now the air between them sizzled. He cupped his palm on the back of her neck, holding her head in place as he explored her mouth. Tasting her lips, her teeth, then brushing soft kisses along her jawline.

"You're so beautiful," he murmured. "Do you have any idea how long I've wanted to taste you?"

He pulled away long enough to meet her eyes, and she actually whimpered from the depth of desire she saw there. A wild, almost violent need. And oh, yes, that's what she wanted. She'd waited too long for this to be polite. At least as long as he had.

"I've wanted you from the first moment I saw you," she confessed. "Remember that day? When I walked into the bar to find my father?"

"How could I forget? It's etched into my memory. You were—you *are*—the most beautiful woman I'd ever seen. I couldn't take my eyes off of you. And I practically had to sit on my hands so I wouldn't reach out and touch you."

Her pulse skittered, and the breath she drew in felt shaky. "You can touch me now," she whispered. And then, because she couldn't stand not having his hands on her, she added, "Please touch me now."

"Oh, babe." She heard the heat in his voice, and she expected his hands on her right away. He surprised her, though, by moving slowly. His fingers trailing lightly over the loose material of her T-shirt.

She'd never thought of a non-touch as being erotic, but the more he didn't touch her, the more aroused she became. Her nipples peaked against the thin material of her bra, and she felt her core go hot. Wet.

And still, that wasn't where he touched her. Instead, he traced the neckline of her shirt, then he followed the seam at her shoulder. He kept his attention on his fingers. On the way they danced along with barely any pressure. Just enough to hint, but not enough to satisfy.

"Please," she whispered, then watched as his fingertip brushed ever so lightly over the swell of her breast. And when he grazed her nipple, she arched back and gasped, then clasped her hand over his, forcing a more solid connection.

"The lady wants it wilder. Harder."

"The lady wants everything," she clarified. "The

lady's not even sure what she wants." Her cheeks warmed. "I'm not very experienced."

He cupped her face. "Elena, are you a virgin?"

She shook her head, glad for her answer, because she had a feeling that he would have backed off if she'd said yes. "I'm not," she said, just to be clear. "But I also haven't been with a lot of guys."

"Never apologize for that," he told her.

"It's just that I don't know—"

"Yeah," he said. "I promise that you do. If you didn't, how do you account for this?"

He took her hand and pressed it against the erection that strained to escape his jeans. She drew in a breath, her body longing for the connection he was offering, but wanting more, too. So much more.

"Is that what you want, Elena?"

"Yes." The answer came without thought or hesitation. "But not yet. First I want—"

He pressed his fingers over her lips. "Let me play," he said. "And if I don't get it just right, you can set me straight, okay?"

She nodded.

"But first, I think we need to move our venue. I don't want to be interrupted when I have you naked and writhing beneath me, do you?"

She swallowed. "No. But you're teasing me."

"Of course I am. But I'm still telling the truth."

She thought of that. Tried to anticipate the pressure of his body on hers. The feel of his cock pressing against her core. The power of the thrust when he found a rhythm and drove it home. She wanted to wake up tomorrow with her thighs aching from being spread so wide, and she wanted to be able to close her eyes and remember what it felt like to be filled by this man.

"What are you thinking?" he asked as they walked to his bedroom.

"That I want you inside me," she said boldly.

"Well, then. I guess it's both our lucky days."

He closed the door, then turned to her. "Take off your clothes."

She lifted a brow, then lifted it higher when he sat

on the foot of the bed his mouth cocked up in a grin. "Go on," he said. "I want to watch."

Instinct told her to decline. But desire made her comply. She wanted to strip for him. Wanted to see the heat build in his eyes. Most of all, she wanted to see the breaking point when he couldn't take it anymore. When he went from watching to touching to taking.

Her heart fluttered. *Yes.* Oh, God, yes. That's what she wanted. To be taken by this man, claimed by him. Worshipped by him.

She lifted her hands to her shoulders, then moved them down, lower and lower as she grazed her fingertips over her collar bone, over the swell of her breasts, over her nipples.

She gasped from her own boldness. From the exotic caress that he was witnessing. But she didn't hesitate, and she didn't close her eyes. And when she finally reached the hem of the shirt, she grasped it between two fingers and gently tugged it up.

It was more awkward than she'd anticipated to take off a shirt slowly, but she never lost control, until finally she stood in front of him in only her bra.

That was when she took one of her fingers, slipped it into her own mouth, then slid the slick finger down inside her jeans, biting her lower lip as she got closer and closer to her core.

"No," he said, and for a moment she thought that he wanted her to stop. Then she realized that she'd started to close her eyes. "Look at me. Eyes right on me."

She did as he said, then saw when the break came. The moment when he couldn't merely watch anymore. When he had to touch her.

She saw it—and she felt the power of it, too. Knowing that she'd compelled him. That his desire for her had propelled him toward her so that now he was on his knees in front of her, his hands at her hips as he drew her jeans down, slowly revealing the tiny pair of cotton panties.

He bent forward, then closed his mouth over her core, sucking her through the cotton and making her gasp from the wildness of it all. "I have to taste you," he said. "All of you." And before she knew it, he had her on her back on the bed, the jeans pulled all the way off, so that she was laid out like a present, wrapped only in a bra and panties.

"Tell me what you want," he said. "Should I get undressed? Or should I undress you?"

She looked at him, still in the jeans and button down he'd worn to work. He looked sexy as hell, and she couldn't wait to see him naked, the hard planes of his chest and abs. And, yes, the hard length of him, evidence that he wanted her.

She wanted that. But she wanted more to be his. Only his. Unwrapped like a present for his pleasure.

She licked her lips, unsure what answer he would prefer, but then she took the plunge and said, "Undress me, Brent."

His slow smile proved to her that she'd made the right choice, and when he bent forward and whispered in her ear, she thought she might just come right then.

"Babe," he murmured, "you have no idea how hard you just made me. But I promise I'll show you soon."

SHE WAS SO DAMN BEAUTIFUL. So damn responsive. And when she'd told him to undress her,

Brent had feared that he was going to come right then.

He'd called on depths of control he didn't even know he had. Anything and everything to keep himself together until he was ready—until they both were. He wanted them on edge. Right on the precipice. And then, yes, he wanted to take her to the stars with him.

All in good time.

Right now, he wanted to taste her, and he started by climbing onto the bed, then straddling her, knowing that the sensation of his clothes against her bare skin would tantalize her, taking her even closer to the edge.

Slowly, he bent forward, then brushed a kiss over her lips. "Close your eyes," he murmured, and when she complied, he gently kissed each eyelid. "Keep them closed," he ordered, then slowly explored the planes of her face with his lips and tongue. The sweet curve of her ear. The texture of her hairline. The elegant curve of her jawline.

Christ, she was lovely.

He nibbled and licked his way down, running his tongue over the curve of her breasts and watching with delight the way she arched up into his touch. Gently, he unfastened the front clasp of her bra, then spread it open, freeing her breasts. Her nipples were hard as pebbles, and she cried out when he closed his mouth over one, sucking hard and then grazing the tight nub with his teeth.

At the same time, he slid his hand down inside her panties, finding her core. "Spread your legs for me, babe," he demanded, and she complied, her hips moving in small circles as if trying to find just the right spot.

But that was his job, and he stroked her slick heat, teasing her clit as he sucked her nipple, his own cock growing rock hard as he played with her, taking her close and making her whimper.

"Please," she murmured, though that was all she said. As if she wanted everything and expected him to deliver.

He intended to.

Without warning, he thrust three fingers inside her, then watched in an erotic haze as she arched up, her body silently begging for more even as her low moans filled the room and teased his cock. He thrust again, slower this time, but deeper, and she rocked against him until they were moving together in the rhythm of sex, and he was growing harder by the minute.

He slipped his fingers free long enough to tug off her panties and toss them aside. Then he closed his hands on her breasts, thumb and forefinger squeezing her nipples as he closed his mouth over her sex. His tongue flicking over her clit, then slipping inside her, tasting her juices, teasing her entrance.

She cried out, begging him to stop, to keep going, to never stop. She rocked her hips, pressing down on him, as if she wanted his tongue deeper, harder. As if she simply wanted him.

That thought was borne out when she cried his name begging him with cries of *please* and *now* but never saying what she wanted.

"Tell me," he ordered. "Tell me what you want."

"You. Please, Brent. I want you."

"Tell me," he repeated.

"I want you inside me. I want your cock. Please, Brent. I want you to fuck me."

"That's my girl," he said, wanting it at least as much as she did. Hell, he didn't remember ever being so hard in his life. And the truth was, though he wanted to prolong the pleasure, he didn't think he could last much longer. He needed to be inside her, and in one swift movement he slid up over her body so that he could reach his bedside table, then pulled out a condom.

He didn't bother getting undressed, just unzipped his pants, took his cock out, and sheathed himself. She was spread wide for him, her core slick and ready. He went slowly, excruciatingly slowly since all his body wanted to do was slam into her, hard and fast. But she needed to be ready, and so he moved slowly and deliberately, building speed and sinking deeper as she grew more ready, until finally she was screaming for him to go faster, to fuck her harder.

And, of course, he had to comply.

She arched up, moving with him, their bodies coming together hard and fast, a desperate coupling as they tried to lose themselves in each other as they exploded into the stars.

"Brent! Oh, God, yes, Brent. Please. Come with me. Come with me now."

He felt the tremors run through her body along with the tightening of her core, the rhythmic spasms that milked him, taking him all the way over the edge with her, until they both shattered, their bodies breaking apart to join the stars, then burning bright before falling slowly, gently back to earth.

He drew in a deep breath, his body limp and spent. But as he drew her close and breathed her scent, he felt the tremors of awareness begin. His body coming back to life. "God, what you do to me," he murmured, reaching around so that he could stroke her as well.

"Looks like you do the same to me," she said, then rolled over and moved him onto his back before straddling him. "I want to go again," she said with a mischievous smile. "And this time I want to ride you."

She got her wish. Two times, actually, which a damn miracle considering the intensity of their lovemaking. But he was spent now, exhausted with sleep pressing down around him.

This was the point when he usually told a woman it was time to go home. But that's not what he said to Elena. Instead, he pulled her close. And all he said was, "Stay."

And, thank God, she did.

Chapter Ten

SOMEHOW HIS REQUEST that she stay on Sunday night had expanded all the way to Tuesday —or, technically, to Wednesday morning, as it was now four in the morning, and she was curled up naked and satisfied next to Brent, who was idly stroking her bare breast with his fingertip.

"Careful," she teased. "You're going to get me all worked up again."

"Wouldn't do you any good," he said. "I think you've broken me."

She laughed, then lightly bit his chest. "That's what I get for sleeping with an older man. No stamina, and—*aaah!*"

The last came out as a strangled squeal when he flipped her over with one quick move, then straddled her, closing his mouth over hers to silence her surprised cry before Faith heard them. But that utilitarian kiss turned immediately wild and deep, and she writhed beneath him as he reached between them, his fingers finding her wet and slippery.

"Never challenge a competitive man," he whispered as he shifted over her body, then slowly entered her.

"I don't know," she managed, the words breathy as her body opened to him, her hips moving in time with his. "I kind of like the consequences."

He laughed, but the sound quickly died as the heat between them built. They clung together, moving slowly at first, then faster as their grip on control faded. She arched up, feeling her body break apart, then clamped her mouth shut and swallowed the scream of ecstasy as a fast, bone-shattering orgasm ripped through her, leaving her breathless and limp, and one-hundred percent convinced that challenging Brent was now her new favorite pastime.

"Careful or you'll kill me," he said when she told him so moments later when he was beside her again, holding her close.

"Can't have that." She rolled over to face him, then sighed with pleasure. "I really should go," she finally said. "I know Faith is wondering why you haven't let her in here before taking her to school the last two days. And as much as I'm enjoying every moment of this, I'm getting shockingly little of my school work done."

"Are you saying I'm a bad influence?"

"The worst," she said, then laughed when he smiled.

"I like the sound of that."

"Ha." She started to slip out of bed, but he took her wrist. "Brent, I'm flattered, but I pay a lot in tuition. I really do have to get my money's worth."

"Not disagreeing. But why don't you come to the bar tonight? It's the Man of the Month contest. Mr. November. We'll have to keep up the just-friends pretense, but it would be nice to see you there. And I'm sure Tyree would love to run his ideas for getting involved in the historical awareness campaign by you."

She sat up, the sheet pulled up over her breasts, which was silly as he'd seen, tasted, and touched every single part of her, with particular emphasis on her breasts. "That sounds like fun. I haven't been to The Fix in days. But unless I pulled a Rip Van Winkle and slept through a decade or so, Faith isn't old enough to stay by herself."

"Which is why she's sleeping over at Kyla's tonight."

"On a school night?"

"Teacher work days tomorrow and Friday, so the kids have holidays. Which means that tonight we have the house to ourselves."

"Oh. *Oh.*" She tossed him a grin, then released a sigh that she hoped sounded suitably exasperated. "Well, I guess that sounds like a good plan."

"Guess? Hmm. Maybe I should give you more of a rundown of the evening's plan. In case you hadn't noticed, we've been spending most of our time behind a locked door. And tonight, we have the whole house."

"Do we?"

"I thought we'd make a late dinner. And I thought I might park you naked on the countertop, spread your legs, and have an appetizer."

"Oh." She swallowed, squeezing her thighs together in response to the heat his words had generated between her legs.

"And of course there's the living room. I thought we'd settle in front of the TV and I'd watch you naked and straddling me, riding me hard as I finger your clit. Unless you'd rather just pop in a movie?"

"Brent…" She squirmed, his words doing naughty, magical things to her body.

"Do you want me to tell you my plan for the backyard? The shower?"

She shook her head. The part of her brain that made words had gone on strike. Her body, however, had not, and she felt raw and tingly, as if he only had to touch her, and she'd explode right then. Her breasts were heavy, her nipples hard. Her sex felt swollen and needy. She wanted his touch—craved it. But when she shifted toward him on the bed, he just moved the opposite direction.

"Sorry, babe. We have to save that for later. You have to get to school."

"You're being incredibly unfair."

He grinned. "I know. I want you thinking about

everything I said all day. And tonight after the contest, we'll come back here." He leaned forward to lightly kiss her. "Wear a dress," he ordered. "Because the first thing I'm going to do when we walk through that door is slide my hand between your legs and see how much you want me."

ELENA WAS giddy when she reached The Fix on Wednesday night. She was running late—she'd gotten stuck on the most amazing phone call—but she was in a fabulous mood.

But the moment she walked stepped over the threshold, giddy morphed into confusion. Griffin stood shirtless on the stage holding a microphone as Beverly stood beside him, looking a little shell shocked. And why not? Griffin never, ever revealed his scars. But he had tonight.

"Buy the calendar if you want to see more," Griffin said, and the unnatural silence that had filled the room was broken by the sound of nervous laughter followed by genuine applause.

"What on earth?" she asked finding Brent, who had a wide smile plastered on his face.

But Brent just shook his head. "He must really love her. Because that was one hell of a grand gesture."

As Jenna bounded onto the stage to announce that Griffin had won the title of Mr. November, Elena cursed softly, hating that she'd missed the actual contest. Then she remembered the reason, and grinned at Brent. "I just had a great meeting. That's why I'm late."

"That's wonderful." She saw him reach for her, then pull his hand back. Her heart twisted, because as much as she was enjoying their time together, it wasn't enough. More and more, she was thinking that she didn't want a secret, temporary thing. She wanted to figure out a way that they could truly be together.

But she also feared that if she told Brent as much, everything would come to an end, including their secret relationship. And she just couldn't risk that.

"Let's go find my dad," she said, using the words as a diversion. "I want to hear about the Food Fair preparations, and make sure he's invited all the historical center big wigs and the local planning commission folks."

"I saw him earlier with Easton," Brent said. "He didn't look happy."

"Bar business?"

"Not sure. I caught his eye, but he didn't call me to the back. But your mom's with him."

"Huh." She frowned, thinking. Easton was a lawyer, but what would her parents need a lawyer for? And if it was about the bar, surely he would have pulled Brent into the conversation.

"Agreed," Brent said when she voiced her thoughts. "Which is why I'm going to go knock on his door. You with me?"

"Should we wait for Reece and Jenna?"

He shook his head. "If it's none of our business, that would look overwhelming and pushy. And if it is about the bar, we can catch them up later."

"Okay," she said, holding tight to the way he'd said *we*.

They maneuvered their way through the bar, then both stopped short when they reached Tyree's office. The door was cracked, and his harsh words slammed into them. "This is bullshit. Total garbage."

"It is," Eva said, her voice soothing. "But let's listen to Easton."

Easton turned, his eyes meeting Elena's through the crack. He gestured for her to come in, though she had to admit that she was no longer certain that she really wanted to walk through those doors.

"Hey," she said tentatively, catching her father's eye. "We didn't mean to eavesdrop. We came to see what was going on with the plans for historical awareness. You know, like we talked about. To get on the Center and the commission's radar."

Tyree snorted. "Oh, we got on their radar, all right."

Eva caught Elena's eye. "He's not upset with you," her mom said, soothing Elena's rising fear before it bubbled over. She longed to hold Brent's hand—something was bad and she didn't want to know what it was—but she wasn't allowed to draw strength from him. Not now. Not in front of these people.

"Daddy?"

Tyree let out a long, frustrated breath, then turned to look at Easton. "I can't even talk about it without putting my fist through a wall. You explain it."

Easton nodded, looking sober. "At the recommendation of the Austin Center for Downtown Conservation and Revitalization and the local historical commission, the city has begun proceedings to forcibly buy The Fix from your father. It's called eminent domain, and it's one of their governmental powers."

"And we can't fucking stop them," Tyree said.

"I didn't say that," Easton put in. "I'll do everything I can. Hannah and I have already started drafting papers to file tomorrow, and we're going to burn up the phone lines making calls and lining up expert witnesses. All I said was that the law specifically allows for eminent domain in order to preserve a historic building as a museum or similar where it appears that the property would otherwise be lost to disrepair or mismanagement. That's not the exact statute, but it's the general idea."

"And from what you say, it's hard to win a challenge to eminent domain."

Easton hesitated, then nodded. "But that doesn't

mean we won't try. And it won't cost you a dime. Hannah wants the money her father left her to fund this. That way it supports you and it filters back into the firm, untainted by her stepfather."

"I can't let you do that."

"You can," Easton said. "But we can talk about that later.

"The vandalism," Brent said, and Elena thought it was as much because he was thinking about the case as that he was trying to divert Tyree from the money situation. "They're using the vandalism as grounds to pursue a forced sale under the statute."

"They are," Easton agreed. "But as we all know— hell, as anyone watching the television show knows —the building is in excellent shape and has recently been improved. That will help our chances."

Tyree didn't seem to hear. He just shook his head.

"It'll be okay, Daddy," Elena said, moving beside him and taking his hand. He pulled her close, hugging her tight.

"Will it?" he asked. "Because from where I'm standing it looks like we worked like hell, got ahead of the game, and now one unexpected play is going to knock us on our asses."

He sighed, his chest rising and falling. "In other words, just when I thought we were in the clear, we're going to lose this whole place after all."

Chapter Eleven

"I'M sorry to put a damper on our plans to have wild sex all over the house," Elena said inside the circle of his arms.

"Oh, baby." He tightened his hold on her. "Don't even worry about it. I'm shell shocked, too."

They were spooned together on his sofa, shifting only to get another sip of wine. They'd already had two glasses each, and the wine had dulled a bit of the shock of Easton and Tyree's announcement.

"Do you think the city will really shut The Fix down?"

He heard real fear in her voice, and though his instinct was to simply reassure her, he owed her the truth. He'd seen a few eminent domain cases play out when he was still a cop—not directly related to his cases, but a few played out tangentially—and he knew that most of the time, the city prevailed.

"It's possible," he said honestly. "But if Landon and I can track down the tagger, maybe we can show the court that the vandalism is under control. That might go a long way to stopping the proceedings."

"That's why they let me go, isn't it? They realized who my father was and knew that this was coming."

He closed his eyes, not wanting to voice the truth that he'd realized back in Tyree's office. "Yeah," he finally said. "I'm pretty sure you're right."

For a moment, she was silent. Then she said, "You'll find them," and the trust in her voice would have brought him to his knees had he not already been stretched out on the couch.

"It's going to be okay," he said, sitting up and pulling her up with him. Without him asking, she shifted, moving to straddle his lap, and for the first time he paid attention to what she was wearing—a black dress with a loose skirt and a fitted bodice closed by a column of tiny, vertical buttons.

"And I'm sorry that the crisis with The Fix over-shadowed your news," he added. She'd told him about an excellent phone meeting with an urban planning consulting firm based in California. Apparently, they already wanted to talk with her about coming on board with them after graduation.

"Thanks," she said, and the pride in her voice did a lot to dull the ache of the knife that news had thrust in his gut. He'd known it would happen—they'd talked about her leaving from day one. He just hadn't expected to be faced with the reality of her departure so soon.

"Hey," she whispered, cupping his stubbled jaw. "Where'd you go?"

"Just thinking about how proud of you I am."

A bright smile lit her face, then faded slightly until she was biting her lower lip, looking both pouty and sexy as hell. "You didn't check," she said, her voice coy. "To see just how much I was thinking of you."

He felt his cock grow hard, and knew from the slight twitch of her eyebrow that she felt it, too. But he swallowed then shook his head a little. "We don't have to, babe. There will be other nights when the house is empty. I know you're upset, and—"

She hushed him with a finger to his lips. "I am. I'm upset and I'm worried and I'm angry. But right now, I just want you to make me forget."

He met her eyes and held her gaze. Then he leaned in, claiming her mouth with his as he slipped his hand inside her skirt, then slowly traced the elastic of her panties before slipping his finger inside the crotch—and swallowing a moan of pleasure and satisfaction at finding her absolutely soaked.

"Make me forget, Brent. Make me forget everything except you."

It was a demand he wouldn't dream of declining, and he teased her through the panties, making her even wetter, until he couldn't stand it anymore, and he had to feel her bare skin. "Take them off," he ordered. "Then unfasten my belt and my jeans."

She grinned, then stood up only long enough to strip off her panties. Then she did as he'd said and focused on the fly of his jeans and his belt. "Lift your hips," she ordered, and he complied, letting her pull them down, then toeing off his shoes so she could pull the jeans and boxers all the way off.

"I like that," she said, seeing how hard he was. She

gave him a seductive look, then with no warning went onto her knees and took him in her mouth.

He groaned, the warm heat of her mouth on his cock driving him crazy. She licked his shaft, alternating licks with sucks, and as she did, she also played with his balls, pushing him right up to the edge, so much so that he couldn't take it any longer. He grasped her head, then guided her motions, amazed and thrilled that she could take him deep, so deep he was amazed he didn't come right then.

Except that wasn't what he wanted. He wanted to be inside her. He wanted to see her face.

"Come here," he said, and she didn't hesitate. She met his eyes, saw what he wanted and climbed onto his lap. He'd had a condom in his pocket earlier, and now it was on the couch—thank God he'd intended to fuck her hard tonight—and he quickly sheathed himself. "Ride me, baby. I don't want to wait. I want you on my lap and my cock inside you."

"Me, too," she said, with such sincerity it almost wrecked him. And then, when she straddled him, her pussy taking in just his tip, he really was afraid he'd lose it.

But he held on, and she impaled herself on him. And together they found the rhythm. Her rising and falling, him guiding her speed and angle with his hands on her hips, until they'd found a perfect rhythm. Until they'd become one. Until they were spiraling up to the heavens together.

Until, finally, they both exploded, shattering in each other's arms before crashing back down to earth and his house and his couch.

Later, when they'd regained their senses, they curled up together under a blanket. "I'm going to take the rest of the week off," he said. "I finalized the hire of the rest of my team before you got there today. Tyree and the other guys can get them rolling," he added, referring to the other part-time member of his security crew.

"How come? So you can try to track down the taggers?"

"That," he admitted. "Plus, since Faith has these two days off, I figure I can stay home with her. Maybe work on that playhouse in the backyard. It's getting a little ratty looking."

"That sounds good," she said. "But why don't we take her out? The children's museum is fun. Or

Innerspace Caverns up in Georgetown. I need to go there to look around the square for my thesis, anyway." The town just north of Austin was host to a series of beautiful underground caverns that had been opened to the public years ago. And the town itself had been founded in the eighteen hundreds and had a charming town square that surrounded the original courthouse.

"Oh, baby, I don't know. I don't want Faith to get her hopes up about you and me."

She shook her head, her expression almost a grimace. "I don't think that would happen. She knows you have female friends. Why would she even be thinking of us as a couple?"

The question made his gut twist, but he forced himself to ignore it. They weren't a couple; they couldn't be a couple. And now more than ever, it was clear that she'd end up moving away.

"Brent?"

"You're right," he said. "We should take her out."

He drew a breath, steeling himself for the upcoming day. Because while an outing with the three of them might not get Faith's hopes up, he knew damn well that he was risking getting his own hopes up.

Chapter Twelve

"LOOK ELENA! I'm painting with light!"

"That's incredible," Elena said, smiling over at Brent, who looked ridiculously proud of his daughter. They were in The Thinkery, a new incarnation of the Austin Children's Museum that none of the three of them had visited before. It was, however, a hit with Faith, who'd checked out every exhibit possible, and even played on the backyard climbing structures.

"One more time, and then we have to go," Brent told her.

"More, Daddy, please?"

He chuckled. "You already got to stay through lunch. Do you want Elena and me to starve?"

She pouted, but didn't argue, and a few moments later she bounced over to them, took each of their hands, and half-walked, half-hung like a monkey as they navigated their way to the exit.

"Hungry!" she announced as soon as they were outside.

"Let's hit Magnolia," Brent suggested. "There's plenty on the menu she'll eat."

"Plenty I'll eat, too," Elena said, her mouth already watering for gingerbread pancakes.

"Can we play again tomorrow?" Faith asked, after they were seated.

Brent caught Elena's eye. "You still want company for your research trip to Georgetown?"

"I think that sounds great."

"Yay!" Faith started clapping. "And can Elena come over for dinner tonight? And can we watch *Tangled*?"

"Yes to dinner," Brent said, "assuming Elena wants to."

"She does," Elena said, making him smile.

"But it's going to be late," he told Faith. "And you're going to be tired. So probably no movie."

"I won't be tired," she said, her voice as serious as a six-year-old could manage. "I'm a big girl now."

"True," Brent said, and like a good dad he didn't remind her later how wrong she was when she fell asleep on the couch only ten short minutes after they'd finished dinner.

"Go take her to bed," Elena said. "I'll clean up."

"Sounds like a deal." He came up behind her, wrapping his arms around her waist and kissing her. "I could get used to this," he said, and she tried very hard not to stiffen in his arms. Because the truth was, she could get used to it, too. But she didn't want to hope. Especially since they'd been so adult about the whole relationship, acknowledging from the inception that it had to be a temporary thing, because she would be leaving.

But what if she didn't have to leave? What if the consulting firm that was courting her had dozens of employees who telecommuted? What if she'd told them that she was only interested in the job if she was among that group?

And what if they'd said yes?

She'd had that conversation yesterday, though she hadn't told Brent. And she didn't intend to. Not yet. Not until it came up naturally. They were still too new. But she was sure—hell she'd never been more sure about anything, or anybody.

She just didn't know if he felt the same.

By the time he came back from reading to Faith, the kitchen was clean. They turned on the television for camouflage noise, then headed back to his room where they made love slowly and sweetly before she settled against him, exhausted from the day and yet energized by the man.

She liked falling asleep with him, but she liked waking up with him even more. Especially on a day like this when they woke up early and showered together. "Oh, no," she said, when he tried to lead her back to bed. "Long day working on my thesis, remember? And playing in Georgetown."

She was right about the long day, too. They alternated between touring the square's historic buildings and taking Faith to places that would amuse her, like the toy shop on the square and the massive park located adjacent to the San Gabriel River. They didn't go to Blue Hole, a local swimming destination, because they hadn't planned ahead with swimsuits. But Faith didn't seem to mind. She was having too much fun playing with the kite they'd bought her on the square and eating a cookie she'd begged for from a local coffee shop.

While Elena watched Faith feed the ducks some stale bread they'd bought from a nearby convenience store, Brent checked in with Landon about the progress of the investigation.

"Anything?" she asked when he settled in next to her.

"Unfortunately, no. Still nothing on the video feeds. And the interviews with nearby employees—waiters, valets, people like that—haven't turned up a thing. Landon's going to assign a detective to interview the homeless, but I'm not holding my breath." He met her eyes. "I think it may be a dead end."

"There has to be a way. If we can't figure it out, my

dad's going to have no defense. He'll lose his business. *Your* business."

"Don't you think I know that?"

She sagged. "I'm sorry. I know you're doing everything you can. I'm just worried."

"I know you are. I am, too. And not just about the business. I worry about you as well."

"Yeah?"

He held her chin and brushed a kiss over her nose. "Yeah. The new cameras are being installed at The Fix today. I'm sending them to your apartment, too. No argument."

"Not making one," she said.

"Good." He hooked an arm around her shoulder. "I want to keep you safe."

And from a man like Brent, she thought, that was almost like saying he loved her.

ELENA AND BRENT spent the next seven days

together, waking up beside each other at his place, then taking Faith to school together before simply hanging out until it was time to pick her up and for Brent to go to work. On the days he didn't go in to The Fix, the three of them often stayed in, cooked dinner, and simply hung out, usually with a children's program on in the background while Elena worked on her thesis and Brent continued to pursue the tagger.

They'd finally stopped trying to hide Elena's presence, but they still didn't tell Faith that Brent and Elena were dating. For that matter, Elena wasn't entirely sure they were dating. She thought so—she hoped so—but she wasn't sure.

Instead, they told Faith that Elena was having work done at her place, so she was staying at Brent and Faith's house. They kept a blanket and pillow on the couch, but even if Faith realized that Elena was in Brent's bed, she doubted that the little girl would think much of it.

The days passed quickly, and whenever Elena went out on her own, her biggest thrill of the day was walking back through those doors. She'd told Selma and Hannah, but only because they'd pried the truth out of her during lunchtime cocktails one day.

"It's real," Selma said. "I mean, you've practically got *serious* stamped on your forehead."

"*I* do, sure," Elena agreed. "But I still don't know where Brent stands."

"Here's an idea," Hannah said. "Ask him."

Elena shot her friend a level look. "Thanks for the tip. I'm working my way up to that." Because if she was wrong, it was all over. She knew that, and she really wasn't ready for it to end.

As if she'd read her mind, Selma put her hand on Elena's shoulder. "It's gonna be fine. The guy's wild about you."

"I've never doubted that," she admitted. "I'm just not sure with Brent if that's going to be enough."

That worry was still on her mind when she swung by The Fix to check on the plans for the Food Fair. Megan and Jenna were the true masterminds behind the event but Elena and Tyree were putting together most of the dishes for The Fix's table by themselves, and running a series of cooking videos on the screen behind their station. She trusted Megan and Jenna, but she still wanted to double-check.

And, besides, that gave her the chance to peek at Brent, and that was never a bad thing. Even though they were still keeping their relationship secret, he flashed a smile at her the moment she walked through the doors. The kind of smile that made her panties damp and promised all sorts of decadent delights come evening.

He was with Tyree, and Elena saw the way her dad looked at him—and the bland way that Brent looked back, neither acknowledging or denying.

She took that as a good sign. Because if Brent was willing to let Tyree get even a hint of a clue that he and Elena were involved, then that had to mean it was serious to him, too.

The thought put a little extra bounce in her step as she headed toward her dad.

"Hi, Daddy. Hi, Brent."

He grinned. "Hi, yourself."

She kept her hands at her sides, fighting the urge to reach for him. "I was just checking in about the fair," she told Tyree. "It's already Thursday, so Saturday is pretty much here. I'm sure Megan and

Jenna are ready, but are we? Any more videos to make? Food to prep? You have servers to work our table?"

Her dad chuckled. "This isn't my first time at the rodeo, *mon bijou*. Your work is done. All you have to do is come on Saturday and enjoy yourself."

"Yeah?"

"And taste the competition's food," he added in a stage whisper. "Gotta know if anyone outshines us."

"Never," she said loyally, then glanced over at Brent. Not because he was part of the conversation, but because she simply couldn't be that close to him and not look at him. "Right. Um, well, okay. I'm going to go run some errands, then."

She leaned forward and pressed a quick kiss to Tyree's cheek. Then she very sternly forced herself not to kiss Brent, as well.

———

"I WANTED TO KISS YOU TODAY."

Brent's words came out of the blue, filling the postcoital silence as they both lay silent and sated after thoroughly exhausting each other.

Elena rolled over, propping herself up on an elbow so that she could see him better. "I think you kissed me a lot," she teased. "And in a lot of very interesting places."

"Funny," he said. "You know what I mean. At The Fix. With your dad."

"Yeah. I know." She met his eyes. "I wanted the same thing."

"Someday," he said, his voice thick with sleep. He took her hand and pulled it to her lips, then kissed her fingertips. "Goodnight, babe," he said, before drifting off.

She kept looking at him, amused. He could do that, just fall off into sleep as easily as stepping off a curb. Not her. Her thoughts kept her awake most nights, and this night was going to be full-on insomnia, but of the best possible kind. Because the thought that filled her mind was the question of what he meant by *someday*.

At the moment, she could only think of good things. And she closed her eyes, smiled, and tried to imagine when exactly *someday* might be.

She was pondering Christmas when she heard the wail. At first she didn't recognize it. Then it hit her that the pitiful cry was coming from Faith's room. She whipped off the sheet, grabbed her robe, and raced down the hall.

The little girl was sitting up in bed, only half-awake, tears streaming down her face.

"Hey! Faith, sweetie, it's okay. I'm here." She hurried to the bed, then climbed on, hugging Faith close to her. "I've got you," she promised as the little girl sobbed against her.

She hiccupped and coughed and slowly calmed down. And then, wrapping her arms tight around Elena's neck, she said, "Mommy."

The word sent a golden spark of pleasure bouncing through her—only to go cold and gray when she turned to see Brent standing in the doorway, his face flat and his eyes empty.

Mommy.

But she wasn't Mommy yet. And in Brent's world, mommies left.

She knew him. Knew the way he thought. Knew his fears about Faith getting attached only to have her heart broken.

Most of all, she knew that this moment was the beginning of the end.

Chapter Thirteen

IT WAS ALL RIGHT THERE in front of him. Everything he craved. Everything he loved.

Everything he was afraid of.

And blinking like a red beacon in the middle of it all was Faith.

Faith.

At the end of the day, she was all that mattered. This wasn't about him. It wasn't about Elena. It was about Faith. About his little girl. A girl whose mommy had walked out on her, and who only had her father now to protect her. To keep the pain at bay. The hurt of being left. Abandoned.

He'd taken on that role when he'd gotten Olivia

pregnant, and he'd renewed the commitment the moment Faith had been put in his arms.

And as much as he wanted Elena—and, oh Christ, he wanted her—he'd sworn never to put Faith in that position again. Never to even risk it.

Elena had known that going into this affair. He had, too.

And he should never have let either of them fall as deep as they had.

"Brent," she said when Faith was finally tucked back in and they'd returned to the living room, both of them knowing by unspoken consent that they couldn't return to his bedroom. Not together, anyway.

It was the first word they'd said to each other since he'd found her and Faith on the bed, and it seemed to hang in the room like a warning. Because, damn him, he wanted to answer her. Wanted to respond not just to his name, but to that tone. A tone that said that she was with him. That she was *his*.

But he couldn't trust it. How the hell could he trust it when he already knew that she was talking with companies on the west coast for jobs when she graduated in two years?

And wouldn't that be great? Two years of getting closer to Faith and then, wham, bam, boom, there she goes.

No.

No way in hell was he doing that to his daughter.

"Brent," she said again. "Listen to me."

"I'm sorry, Elena. I'm so damn sorry, but we both knew this wasn't permanent."

"Maybe I want it to be." She looked defiantly into his eyes, and his heart twisted as his resolve weakened. But no. *No.*

He drew in a breath. "It's not about what you want. Hell, it's not about what I want. It's not even about what Faith wants. It's about what's best for her. And Elena, that's not you. It can't be you, because we both know you're going away."

"No," she said earnestly, "I'm not." She drew in a breath and pressed her fingers to her temples before perching on the edge of the sofa, looking a bit like a lost little girl herself in the old robe of his that he'd given her.

When she lifted her head, he saw pain in her eyes, and he hated that he was the one who put it there. But there would be pain—that was inevitable. And it was his job to see that it wasn't Faith who suffered.

"Listen to me, Brent. I'm not going anywhere. I was planning to tell you tomorrow. I made up my mind. I'm staying right here."

He flinched, his brow furrowing as he tried to make sense of her words.

"I get it, you know. I understand what you're doing for Faith, and I get it. Hell, I agree with it. I grew up without a father, remember? I understand what you're trying to protect. And because I do, I decided to stay."

He said nothing, but he sat in the chair opposite her.

She licked her lips and plowed on. "I love you," she said, and instead of settling over him warm and soft, the words seemed to burn through him, leaving painful scars that seared his soul.

"And I know you're going to say I'm too young," she continued, "but I'm certain of it."

"Elena—"

"*No.*" She cut him off sharply. "Dammit, Brent, I want a chance. You don't have to say you love me back right away," she added, and the fact of his love sat heavy inside him.

"But I know that you do," she continued. "I can feel it, Brent, and I know you can, too. And … well, because of that, I've been looking at only certain jobs. Ones that are either here or that will let me work from here. There are lots of opportunities. I don't have to go away to do what I want. You're afraid of stealing my dream, and I get that. But you aren't. And you're afraid that I'll change my mind and steal Faith's heart. But you're wrong. I won't. I'm staying. For the work. And because I love you."

She sat back, her expression tight, almost exhausted. "Please," she added softly. "Please say something."

"I can't take the risk," he said, forcing the words out. "She'll only remember tonight as a dream. Won't even know what she called you. But it doesn't matter. That feeling is already inside her. It's going to be hard enough having you leave as a friend. I can't risk her mother walking away."

"I told you." Her words came out clipped, bordering on angry. "I'm not going to."

"You say that now, but you're not even out of graduate school. Things change, Elena."

"Don't you treat me like a child." The words snapped and crackled, alive with fury. "I'm not Olivia, dammit. And you need to stop looking for her around every corner. Brent, please," she added, her tone softening. "Don't deny yourself or Faith a relationship just because you're scared."

A cold hand tightened around his heart, and his mouth went dry. But all he did was shake his head. "I think you need to go now."

"Brent. Please."

"I'm sorry. But you need to go."

ELENA DIDN'T WANT to talk to anyone, much less Hannah or Selma, who were so happy with their men and had been so convinced that she'd find happiness with Brent.

She had found it—and he'd tossed it all away. He thought he was protecting Faith; she knew that. But he wasn't. All he was doing was putting a Band-Aid over the wound Olivia had inflicted.

He'd never find a woman he trusted to stay, mostly because he didn't believe anyone would stay. He'd been burned, and the only one who could make him get over it was him.

Which was all very profound and reasonable, but what the hell was she supposed to do now? She loved him. Did she just walk away? Did she fight, even if fighting was futile?

Did she keep crying into her pillow and watching sappy romances that left her bawling at the end?

No, she told herself firmly, *she did not.*

Instead she hauled her butt off the bed, then marched to the bathroom where she showered, brushed her teeth, and put on enough makeup to feel human again.

Then she grabbed her purse and her car keys and headed for her parents' house.

Of course, it wasn't them she wanted to see. She already knew that Tyree thought Brent was too old for her, and loaded with a bit of baggage called Faith. Her mom might have a different perspective, but Elena wasn't inclined to risk it.

Still, it didn't matter. They were both at The Fix. Her mom was shooting Matthew and Griffin for the calendar, and her dad was there meeting with Easton about the eminent domain action.

No, it wasn't them she wanted to see. She was looking for Eli. He might only be sixteen, but they'd had some long talks about their parents. He'd lost his mom when he was young, and they'd bonded over their shared blood and odd parental situations.

He might not have advice, but he was a shoulder to cry on. And at that moment she was tired of crying on pillows.

He was fortunately home, and when she'd called him from the car to give him the quick rundown, he'd told her to come on over.

Now he pulled open the door just a few seconds after she rang the bell. "Wow," he said, "you said you felt like shit, and you look like it, too."

"And to think that most of my life I didn't realize what I was missing by not having a little brother."

He snorted, and she followed him inside. "I really am sorry," he said when they settled at the kitchen table. "I mean, breakups suck."

"That they do."

"So, what can I do?"

"Honestly? I don't know. I just wanted someone to talk to. Which I did over the phone. Any brilliant advice come your way while I was making the drive over here?"

"Yeah, but you're not gonna like it."

"What?"

"Talk to Dad. Nobody knows Brent better than he does except Jenna and Reece. So I guess that's my advice, too. Talk to them."

She'd considered it, but she happened to know they were hard at work on the baby's room, and she hated to interrupt for her own relationship angst.

"Then Dad's your best bet," Eli said, after she told him as much.

"He'll just say that I was stupid to get involved with an older man."

"Were you?"

"No," she said indignantly. "Our ages aren't the problem. It's that bitch Olivia. She poisoned him."

"So argue with Dad. He'll put up a fight, but he'll come around if you're right. And maybe he'll have some advice. Or at least you'll have another shoulder, right?"

She couldn't help but smile.

"Listen, I'm really sorry, but while you were on your way over, the hospital called. And you know that internship I've got? Well, they need me to come in because someone else called out sick."

"Oh, yeah. Go. I don't want to hold you up."

"You can hang for as long as you want. We've got cheesecake in the fridge. My mom always used to eat cheesecake when she was sad."

"I think I would have liked your mom."

"Yeah? Well, we're even then, because I like yours."

"I got lucky in the little brother department," she said, giving him a hug.

"Here's hoping you get lucky in the Brent department, too," he said, then headed for the door. "Talk to you later, okay?"

"Sounds good. And thanks."

And then, just like that, she was alone again, her thoughts once again on Brent and her longing and her inability to get even an ounce of reason through his thick skull.

Damn the man.

With a sigh, she headed for the fridge. She was about to undertake a little cheesecake therapy when she heard the key in the lock. Then the kitchen door opened and Tyrec stepped in.

"Ah, *mon bijou.* What a surprise. Oh, baby, no," he added when she burst into tears. "What's wrong?"

"I don't want to talk about it. Where's Mom?"

"She's shopping. You don't want to talk about it with me? Or you don't want to talk about it at all?"

She peered at him through a liquid film, but didn't answer.

"So it's about Brent, then. Well, I wouldn't want to talk about it with me, either."

She lifted her head and sniffed noisily.

He went to the pantry, opened the door, then pulled an apron off a hook. He handed it to her, and she took it out of reflex.

"What—"

"Come cook with me."

"But—will it help?"

"Is there anything you can do right now to fix whatever happened between you two?"

"No."

"Is there anything you can tell me that will make it all feel better?"

Again, she shook her head.

"In that case, *ma cherie,* it seems that cooking's about the only thing we can do."

She considered that, nodded, then tied the apron around her waist. It might not help, but it damn sure couldn't hurt. And right then, she really did want her dad.

Chapter Fourteen

BRENT HAD BEEN LIVING in a fog since Thursday, certain he'd done the right thing, and yet feeling that certainty buckle under his feet every time he thought of her and every time Faith asked when Elena would be coming over.

Dammit, he knew what he knew. And what he knew was that he'd made the right decision.

But if that was so, why did he feel so hollow? And why was he second-guessing himself in every quiet moment.

And why did he keep picking up his phone to dial her number only to toss the damn thing away.

Because he missed her. Plain and simple. He could admit it. It was true, after all.

But just because he missed her didn't mean he should open his world to her. That he should risk Faith's stability and happiness.

Doubts niggled at him, pushing at him in soft moments, filling his head when he was idle. So he tried not to be idle, and he was thankful when Saturday night rolled around and he could occupy himself with getting ready for the Food Fair while Faith stayed the night at Kyla's house.

It was black tie, and as he tied his bowtie, he couldn't help but wonder what she was wearing.

For that matter, he couldn't help but wonder if she was going.

He hoped she was. If nothing else, he wanted to talk with her.

He wanted it enough, actually, that he arrived fifteen minutes early, using his connection to The Fix to get inside. He heard her voice, then immediately felt his pulse kick up, but it was only the video of her and Tyree making lasagna rolls.

He watched for a few moments, memorizing the

features he already knew so well, remembering the sensation of her velvet skin against his fingers, her soft lips upon his neck. *Elena.*

"Hello, Brent."

His entire body tensed, and he stayed perfectly still, telling himself it was only his imagination. But he knew better, and he slowly turned around to face her.

"Hello, Elena. You look lovely." She wore a long, almost sheer beaded gown that showed off her height and her lean figure.

"You're not too bad yourself."

He tried to speak, then had to try a second time as his mouth was too dry. "Can we talk?"

"I guess that's up to you."

He nodded. "I deserved that. But listen. I want— well, the truth is I miss you."

He saw a spark in those lovely eyes.

"And I wanted you to know that I still want to be friends."

The spark dimmed. And his heart beat five times

before she finally answered him.

"I can't," she said. "I'm an all or nothing kind of woman, Brent. And the truth is that I love you. And I want it all. I suppose I should have said it before, but I'm telling you now. I love you," she repeated. "I'm certain of it. Desperately, hopelessly. And I'm sorry if the news makes you uncomfortable, but that's just the way it is." She drew a breath, and when she did, he remembered to breathe as well.

She loved him.

"I'm sorry if you don't love me, too, because I can't imagine finding anyone to fill my heart the way you and Faith do."

You and Faith.

It had just come out, but she meant it. He could tell. She wanted him. But she wanted the family, too. Faith wasn't an afterthought. The boyfriend's annoying attachment. She truly wanted the entire package.

And, damn him, he was still too fucking scared to take the risk.

"Brent?"

His throat felt tight. "It really was good to see you," he said lamely.

She held his eyes, and he saw tears well in hers. "Well. I guess. I guess I should go mingle."

"Elena, wait—" But she'd faded back into the crowd. And he was left standing there feeling like he was a sixteen-year-old boy all over again.

He wandered through the fair, only half looking at the lovely serving tables, and not even tasting the exquisite food. All he wanted was to find her. To tell her that he was an idiot.

To tell her that now he was willing to take the risk.

From across the room, Jenna made a beeline toward him. "You look like hell. Have you caught something?"

"I think so. I'm going to head home."

She pressed her palm to his forehead. "You're not warm, but that's probably a good idea. I hope it wasn't something you ate. I'd hate to think we're going to have an outbreak of food poisoning after this event."

"I haven't eaten a bite."

She looked so relieved he had to laugh. After a moment, she joined in. "Sorry," she said. "Just … you know."

"Yeah. I do. I'm looking for Elena," he said after a moment had passed.

"Trouble in paradise?"

He cocked his head. "You knew?"

"Duh. And all I'm going to say now is that you two are perfect together. Take it under advisement."

"Thanks for the tip."

"And if you're looking for her, your best bet is Tyree."

Since that made sense, he left her by a cake ball table and went in search of Tyree. He found him near the bar, a glass of scotch in one hand.

"I had a long talk with my daughter recently," Tyree said without preamble. "And she says you make her happy. Since I've seen the way you two look at each other, I believe it. So why isn't she on your arm right now?"

He started to say that Elena wasn't with him

because he'd been an idiot, but before he could, Tyree continued.

"I'll tell you why. Because you're living with the shadow of Olivia. But that woman was a terrible wife and a horrible mother. Maybe she was a bad person. I don't know. I never knew her that well. But I know she was weak. And don't you dare judge Elena next to her. Give the girl some credit. You think she's just going to abandon her dreams? No. But you're part of those dreams now. So she'll figure out a way to work all of her plans together. Better yet, you two can work it out together."

"I'm older than she is." Brent said, his mood improving now that he knew Tyree had come around and now supported his plan to claim Elena.

"You don't say."

"That doesn't bother you?"

"Turns out I'm not a key variable in this equation. The relevant question is, does it bother you?"

"No."

"There you go. She's always gonna be my little girl. But I know you, Brent. I know you better than most anybody except Reece and Jenna. And I couldn't ask for a better son-in-law. Or am I presuming?"

Brent didn't even miss a beat. "No, sir," he said.

"Then I think you have somewhere to be right now."

"I would, if I knew where she was."

"She went home," Tyree told him. "You go see her tonight. Tomorrow, we'll talk about this eminent domain bullshit."

"Good. Because Landon and I've been—"

"Sir?" A lanky man in a Winston Hotel uniform held out an envelope. "You're Tyree Johnson?"

"Yes."

"This arrived for you by messenger."

"Thank you." Tyree tipped the man, then started to open the note.

"I'll talk to you tomorrow," Brent said, assuming it was a love note from Eva setting up a tryst in one of the hotel rooms.

"*Wait.*" Tyree reached out and grabbed Brent's arm, his voice strangled.

"What?" Fingers of dread crawled up his spine. "What happened?"

Tyree didn't answer. Just handed him the note.

We know how to get you where it hurts.

Call off your bloodhounds and quit fighting the action. If not, it will be worse for her next time.

Brent felt the blood drain from his face.

"Elena," Tyree said.

But Brent was already racing for his car, and Tyree followed, right on his heels.

Chapter Fifteen

"FASTER," Tyree yelled as Brent floored the Volvo while shouting at Landon over the car's speakerphone system.

"I've got two black and whites racing to her apartment," Landon said. "And I've put out a call that you not be pulled over. She'll be fine, you two. Just hang in there."

Brent nodded. He knew she would be. Any other reality was unacceptable. "I was right about Bodacious," he said. "And damn me, I could have nailed the bastard days ago if I'd only made the connection when the Center cut Elena loose."

"I'll follow up whatever lead you want, but you're going to have to run that one by me more slowly."

"The Fix is a prime location, right? And the folks from Bodacious have been trying to get their hands on it for ages. That's why Ted Henry called Tyree's loan," Brent said, referring to the man who'd lent Tyree the money to open the bar, then later invested heavily in the corporation that owned Bodacious. "He wanted Tyree to default so he could foreclose on the property."

Ted Henry was actually the impetus behind the Man of the Month contest. Tyree needed cash to pay off the note, so Reece and Brent invested. But Tyree insisted the bar be in the black and debt free by the end of the year. And Jenna had come up with the brilliant—and lucrative—idea of the contest to increase revenue.

"So even though Ted Henry was out of luck, the folks from Bodacious just kept trying. Stiff competition. Poaching employees. Graffiti. Vandalism. But nothing worked. They didn't shake Tyree from The Fix at all."

"And then someone must have realized that if they couldn't get the property, then getting it away from Tyree was the next best thing," Landon said, picking up the thread.

"How does this fit in with Elena?" Tyree asked.

"Someone from Bodacious must be involved with the Center," Brent said. "And when they set the plan in motion they didn't realize who she was— your daughter, I mean. Obviously, she had to go before she put two and two together."

"We find the person with a link to the Center and to Bodacious, and we have our perp," Landon said. "I'm on it."

"We have more," Brent added. "I doubt they realize her apartment has security cameras. Pull the feed, and I bet you have a face."

"On that, too," Landon said. "You two just focus on Elena."

"That's the plan," Brent said. "After all, I'm not a cop anymore."

He ended the call just as he made a hard right into her apartment driveway. The patrol cars had beat them there, and the complex was bathed in the eerie red and blue strobe of police lights.

"Come on," he said to Tyree, though words were unnecessary. His friend was already out of the car and racing toward her unit.

"She's okay, sir," a uniformed officer told him. "Detective Landon said to give you full access."

"Thanks." They passed the cop and stepped into what looked like a blood-soaked living room.

"Paint," another officer said. "Thrown in through the windows."

"And Elena?" Brent demanded.

"Fine. She's giving a statement. She'll be done shortly. They didn't touch the bedroom. Apparently, she slept through it all."

He nodded, unsurprised. Considering their encounter at the fair, he imagined she'd had a few drinks before going to bed.

"Did they enter the premises, or just throw the paint cans in?"

"We've got them entering, sir," the officer said. "They sprayed a message on the bathroom mirror. *Next time it will be her.*"

Brent's insides knotted and he met Tyree's rage-filled eyes. Yeah, Landon was *so* going to nail these bastards. And then Brent was going to dance at their sentencing.

"Brent! Daddy!"

Elena stumbled out of her bedroom and into Tyree's arms. For a moment, Brent felt lost, afraid that she was going to shun him, not give him the chance to apologize.

But then she pulled away, and Tyree stepped back. "Talk you two. I'll be outside when you need me."

"You came," she whispered once Tyree had gone.

"Of course I came." He guided her to a quiet corner of the dining room. "You're alright? Can I touch you? I need to touch you. We know who did this. Landon's on it. But I have to touch you now."

"Yes, please. Brent, I'm so—I'm sorry. I don't want to lose you, and if the only way I can have you in my life is to be your friend, then I can handle that. I won't like it, but I can—"

"Marry me."

She blinked at him. "What?"

"You heard me. I want you to marry me."

"Wait. No. What? Because some guy attacked my apartment?"

"No, because I love you. I was on my way from the Food Fair to tell you— to ask you—before I knew about any of this. Ask Tyree."

Her face brightened. "Truly?"

"I swear on my daughter's life."

"Oh." Her voice was soft. Reverent. She understood too well what Faith meant to him. "Brent." She touched his cheek. "But why? Why marriage? Why so fast?"

"Because I'm miserable without you. Because I believe that you love me too. And don't say it's too fast, because dammit, Elena, I know. *I know*. And I think you do, too. But if you want to wait, that's fine, too. We can wait forever, because I know you're not going anywhere. And neither am I."

"That was a great speech. Did you rehearse it?"

"Not a word."

She laughed. "I love you, Brent Sinclair."

"Is that a yes?"

"That's a yes. On two conditions."

"Anything."

"I want to adopt Faith. You want me in her life. I want to be her mother. Assuming she wants that too."

"Oh, babe." If he wasn't already in love with her, he would have fallen hard right then. And since he already had a court order terminating Olivia's parental rights, they could make that happen right away.

"That would make me very happy," he continued. "And I'm sure Faith wants you as much as I do." He took her hand. "What else?"

"All my friends have boyfriends or husbands who are in the Man of the Month calendar. The Mr. December contest is next week." She flashed a mischievous grin. "I want you to enter it. Bonus points if you win."

"Good God. Really?" He stepped closer. "And what's my bonus?"

"I'd show you, but these nice men might not want to see me naked."

He laughed then pulled her close. "All right. I'll win

the contest. And then I'll marry you. And then we'll live happily ever after. How does that sound?"

She wrapped her arms around his neck and smiled at him, her eyes full of warmth and tenderness and love. "I think that sounds just about perfect."

Epilogue

"EVERYBODY!" Tyree stood on the stage and thrust up his hands. "Hey, can I have everyone's attention, please?"

All around him, the friends, co-workers, and customers who'd come for The Fix on Sixth New Year's Eve bash continued to talk and laugh and drink as the clock ticked its way toward midnight.

"Hang on," Taylor said. She stood just a few feet away holding Landon's hand, and the two of them were among the few who were actually listening. She released Landon long enough to trot to the locked cabinet that was camouflaged into the exterior wall. She punched in the code, pulled out a cordless mike, fiddled with the settings, then hurried back to Tyree. "You're all set," she said as she handed it to him.

Tyree shot her a grateful smile, then lifted the mike to his mouth. He flipped it on, then said hesitantly. "Can y'all hear me?"

His voice boomed out through the recently upgraded speaker system, and a chorus of "yes!" accompanied by applause filled the bar's main room.

He'd rehearsed tonight's speech, but for a moment, he feared that he would forget it as he looked out at all the people who were looking back at him. But then he reminded himself that these were his friends. His customers. Hell, they were his family. And remembering that, his nerves faded, and he flashed a broad, happy grin at the crowd.

"First of all, I want to thank you all for coming. As some of you know, this New Year's Eve party is a tradition at The Fix. But this year it's extra special, because a few months ago, I'd been afraid that we were going to have to shut this place down by the end of the year."

A chorus of boos and "no way!" echoed through the room.

"Well, you're right," Tyree continued. "Because I have some brilliant and generous folks working with me. Jenna, Brent, Reece, you three need to take a bow. We not only infused some capital back into this place, but we launched the Man of the Month contest, which pulled us back firmly into the black."

Another explosion of applause, and Tyree's grin grew wide.

"Not to mention a reality show," he added, as someone in the crowd lifted Brooke up above the sea of faces as she laughed and squealed in protest.

"And of course most of you know about Brent and Easton and Landon's heroic and successful work in thwarting an attempt to use the city's power of eminent domain to shut us down. We couldn't have foiled that without lawyers and cops—who happen to be customers—working together."

They'd caught the vandals, who'd ratted out the higher ups at Bodacious, including Ted Henry and the local Bodacious manager, Steven Kane. Easton had used that evidence to challenge the eminent domain action, proving that absent those crimes, The Fix was being well-cared for. Seeing the writing on the wall, the city had withdrawn the action.

In front of Tyree, Taylor hugged Landon while Brent gave Easton a congratulatory slap on the back just seconds before Selma pulled him down for a messy kiss, and Elena moved in to hug Brent, her diamond engagement ring shining.

"In other words," Tyree continued, "it's been quite a year. And I'm looking forward to many, many more."

Once again, glasses were raised along with congratulatory voices.

There were still a few minutes left, so he told the crowd about the calendars and cookbooks, then went around the room, pointing at each of the calendar models and introducing them to the crowd, starting with Mr. January, Reece, who stood by the bar next to Jenna, who looked ready to pop any minute. Hard to believe she still had most of the month to go.

And then there was Spencer—Mr. February—who was sharing a bottle of wine with Brooke and their cameramen, Nick and Casper were their nicknames —Tyree never did learn their real ones. The four had moved from filming *The Business Plan* at The Fix to filming *Mansion Makeover* at the old Drysdale

Mansion that Brooke and Spencer both occupied and were in the process of renovating.

Mr. March, Cam, was working behind the bar, moving at a speed that would have intimidated a lesser man. His girlfriend Mina and her brother, Darryl, sat on the stools in front of him, their attention split between Cam and Tyree.

It took Tyree a second to find Mr. April, but then he saw the group in the corner, with Nolan in the center telling what appeared to be a raucous joke as Shelby looked on, both amused and appalled.

Of course, he had to introduce himself as Mr. May, then he continued to navigate around the room, finding Mr. June, Parker at the bar with Megan talking to Mr. July, Derek, and his girlfriend Amanda.

August was easy, as Landon and Taylor were right by the stage, and Landon took a bow with sportsman-like grace.

Misters September and October—Tyree's lawyer, Easton, and his personal trainer, Matthew—stood together with their girlfriends, Selma and Hannah. It took a moment for Tyree to find Griffin, Mr. November, in the audience; he was so used to looking for the writer and voice actor's gray hoodie that he almost missed the man who sat with Beverly, his movie star girlfriend, at one of the tables with absolutely nothing covering the violent burn scars on his face or arm.

Tears of pride welled in his throat, as intense as if Griffin were his own son, and his voice shook a little as he moved onto Mr. December, his soon to be son-in-law, Brent, who had won the contest by a landslide.

On the big screen TV, episodes of *The Business Plan* were playing on a loop. In just a few minutes, the screen would go dark, and then a countdown would mark time to the new year. But until then, Tyree was going to enjoy what remained of this one. It had been one hell of a ride, but ultimately one hell of a good year.

A few feet away, Eva started toward him, her smile lighting his soul. *Yeah*, he thought. *One hell of a good year.*

He reached out a hand and drew her up onto the stage with him, his eyes seeking out Elena who beamed at both of them.

As soon as Eva was beside him, he pulled her tight

against him, dipped her, and kissed her soundly, making her laugh and the entire room burst into applause.

"Thank you, everybody," he called out, speaking once again into the mike. "You've made the first six years of The Fix a raging success. We had some rocky ground, but I think we proved that there's nothing more magical than friendship—and love," he added, once more hugging Eva to his side.

"Well, said," Brent called out, as Elena clapped and Reece let loose with a wolf whistle.

"Champagne and wine are complimentary, as are the taxis and ride shares for anyone who overindulges. And we have one free calendar for every guest, but feel free to buy lots of extras for your friends," he added, making the crowd laugh again.

"Congratulations again, Daddy," Elena said, giving him a huge hug as he descended the steps with Eva at his side. "Right back at you, *mon bijou*. And let me see this *bijou*," he said, peering at her engagement ring. He hooked an arm around both Elena and Brent. "Take care of each other," he said. "You know I love you both."

"We know," Elena said, and as she smiled at Brent, Tyree noticed a tall man with silver hair striding toward them. He frowned, trying to place the face, but not succeeding.

"Brent. You know this guy?"

"Looks familiar, but I'm not—*oh.*"

But Brent didn't need to tell Tyree who the man was, as he came right up and introduced himself. "Thomas Baker," he said. "And you must be Tyree Johnson."

"I am. What can I do for you? I hope you're enjoying the party."

"It's excellent. This is a good business you've built up here."

Something in his tone caught Tyree's attention, and he cocked his head, trying to read the man. "What brings you here tonight?"

"Honestly? I came because I owe you an apology."

"How so?"

"Baker Holdings owns Bodacious," he said. "And I understand some of my employees and investors got carried away in the worst possible way. I just wanted you to know that we're cooperating with the police regarding the prosecution. I've spoken to the staff at the Sixth Street Bodacious, and I've put in new management. Better trained management."

"Oh." Tyree wasn't sure how to respond.

"At any rate, that's the apology. In addition, I wanted to say that I'm impressed with what you've accomplished this year. I'm proud to be your competition, and sorry again about the shenanigans."

"No hard feelings," Tyree said. "There's enough business to go around."

"Damn right," Baker said. "But if you ever do decide to sell…"

Tyree looked around at the room filled with his friends and customers. More important, filled with love and laughter.

"Sorry, Mr. Baker," he said as the countdown to midnight began. "But The Fix is my home, full of my family. And so I'm holding on tight to this place, and I'm never letting go."

Are you eager to learn which Man of the Month book features which sexy hero? Here's a handy list!

Down On Me - meet Reece

Hold On Tight - meet Spencer

Need You Now - meet Cameron

Start Me Up - meet Nolan

Get It On - meet Tyree

In Your Eyes - meet Parker

Turn Me On - meet Derek

Shake It Up - meet Landon

All Night Long - meet Easton

In Too Deep - meet Matthew

Light My Fire - meet Griffin

Walk The Line - meet Brent

&

Bar Bites: A Man of the Month Cookbook

Down On Me excerpt

Did you miss book one in the Man of the Month series? Here's an excerpt from Down On Me!

Chapter One

Reece Walker ran his palms over the slick, soapy ass of the woman in his arms and knew that he was going straight to hell.

Not because he'd slept with a woman he barely knew. Not because he'd enticed her into bed with a series of well-timed bourbons and particularly inventive half-truths. Not even because he'd lied to his best friend Brent about why Reece couldn't drive with him to the airport to pick up Jenna, the third player in their trifecta of lifelong friendship.

No, Reece was staring at the fiery pit because he was a lame, horny asshole without the balls to tell the naked beauty standing in the shower with him that she wasn't the woman he'd been thinking about for the last four hours.

And if that wasn't one of the pathways to hell, it damn sure ought to be.

He let out a sigh of frustration, and Megan tilted her head, one eyebrow rising in question as she slid her hand down to stroke his cock, which was demonstrating no guilt whatsoever about the whole going to hell issue. "Am I boring you?"

"Hardly." That, at least, was the truth. He felt like a prick, yes. But he was a well-satisfied one. "I was just thinking that you're beautiful."

She smiled, looking both shy and pleased—and Reece felt even more like a heel. What the devil was wrong with him? She *was* beautiful. And hot and funny and easy to talk to. Not to mention good in bed.

But she wasn't Jenna, which was a ridiculous comparison. Because Megan qualified as fair game, whereas Jenna was one of his two best friends. She trusted him. Loved him. And despite the way his cock perked up at the thought of doing all sorts of delicious things with her in bed, Reece knew damn well that would never happen. No way was he risking their friendship. Besides, Jenna didn't love him like that. Never had, never would.

And that—plus about a billion more reasons—meant that Jenna was entirely off-limits.

Too bad his vivid imagination hadn't yet gotten the memo.

Fuck it.

He tightened his grip, squeezing Megan's perfect rear. "Forget the shower," he murmured. "I'm taking you back to bed." He needed this. Wild. Hot. Demanding. And dirty enough to keep him from thinking.

Hell, he'd scorch the earth if that's what it took to burn Jenna from his mind—and he'd leave Megan limp, whimpering, and very, very satisfied. His guilt. Her pleasure. At least it would be a win for one of them.

And who knows? Maybe he'd manage to fuck the fantasies of his best friend right out of his head.

It didn't work.

Reece sprawled on his back, eyes closed, as Megan's gentle fingers traced the intricate outline of the tattoos inked across his pecs and down his arms. Her touch was warm and tender, in stark contrast to the way he'd just fucked her—a little too wild, a little too hard, as if he were fighting a battle, not making love.

Well, that was true, wasn't it?

But it was a battle he'd lost. Victory would have brought oblivion. Yet here he was, a naked woman beside him, and his thoughts still on Jenna, as wild and intense and impossible as they'd been since that night eight months ago when the earth had shifted beneath him, and he'd let himself look at her as a woman and not as a friend.

One breathtaking, transformative night, and Jenna didn't even realize it. And he'd be damned if he'd ever let her figure it out.

Beside him, Megan continued her exploration, one fingertip tracing the outline of a star. "No names? No wife or girlfriend's initials hidden in the design?"

He turned his head sharply, and she burst out laughing.

"Oh, don't look at me like that." She pulled the sheet up to cover her breasts as she rose to her knees beside him. "I'm just making conversation. No hidden agenda at all. Believe me, the last thing I'm interested in is a relationship." She scooted away, then sat on the edge of the bed, giving him an enticing view of her bare back. "I don't even do overnights."

As if to prove her point, she bent over, grabbed her bra off the floor, and started getting dressed.

"Then that's one more thing we have in common." He pushed himself up, rested his back against the headboard, and enjoyed the view as she wiggled into her jeans.

"Good," she said, with such force that he knew she meant it, and for a moment he wondered what had soured her on relationships.

As for himself, he hadn't soured so much as fizzled. He'd had a few serious girlfriends over the years, but it never worked out. No matter how good it started, invariably the relationship crumbled. Eventually, he had to acknowledge that he simply wasn't relationship material. But that didn't mean he was a monk, the last eight months notwithstanding.

She put on her blouse and glanced around, then slipped her feet into her shoes. Taking the hint, he got up and pulled on his jeans and T-shirt. "Yes?" he asked, noticing the way she was eying him speculatively.

"The truth is, I was starting to think you might be in a relationship."

"What? Why?"

She shrugged. "You were so quiet there for a while, I wondered if maybe I'd misjudged you. I thought you might be married and feeling guilty."

Guilty.

The word rattled around in his head, and he groaned. "Yeah, you could say that."

"Oh, *hell.* Seriously?"

"No," he said hurriedly. "Not that. I'm not cheating on my non-existent wife. I wouldn't. Not ever." Not in small part because Reece wouldn't ever have a wife since he thought the institution of marriage was a crock, but he didn't see the need to explain that to Megan.

"But as for guilt?" he continued. "Yeah, tonight I've got that in spades."

She relaxed slightly. "Hmm. Well, sorry about the guilt, but I'm glad about the rest. I have rules, and I consider myself a good judge of character. It makes me cranky when I'm wrong."

"Wouldn't want to make you cranky."

"Oh, you really wouldn't. I can be a total bitch." She sat on the edge of the bed and watched as he tugged on his boots. "But if you're not hiding a wife in your attic, what are you feeling guilty about? I assure you, if it has anything to do with my satisfaction, you needn't feel guilty at all." She flashed a mischievous grin, and he couldn't help but smile back. He hadn't invited a woman into his bed for eight long months. At least he'd had the good fortune to pick one he actually liked.

"It's just that I'm a crappy friend," he admitted.

"I doubt that's true."

"Oh, it is," he assured her as he tucked his wallet into his back pocket. The irony, of course, was that

as far as Jenna knew, he was an excellent friend.
The best. One of her two pseudo-brothers with
whom she'd sworn a blood oath the summer after
sixth grade, almost twenty years ago.

From Jenna's perspective, Reece was at least as good
as Brent, even if the latter scored bonus points
because he was picking Jenna up at the airport
while Reece was trying to fuck his personal demons
into oblivion. Trying anything, in fact, that would
exorcise the memory of how she'd clung to him that
night, her curves enticing and her breath intoxicating, and not just because of the scent of too much
alcohol.

She'd trusted him to be the white knight, her noble
rescuer, and all he'd been able to think about was
the feel of her body, soft and warm against his, as
he carried her up the stairs to her apartment.

A wild craving had hit him that night, like a tidal
wave of emotion crashing over him, washing away
the outer shell of friendship and leaving nothing but
raw desire and a longing so potent it nearly brought
him to his knees.

It had taken all his strength to keep his distance
when the only thing he'd wanted was to cover

every inch of her naked body with kisses. To stroke her skin and watch her writhe with pleasure.

He'd won a hard-fought battle when he reined in his desire that night. But his victory wasn't without its wounds. She'd pierced his heart when she'd drifted to sleep in his arms, whispering that she loved him—and he knew that she meant it only as a friend.

More than that, he knew that he was the biggest asshole to ever walk the earth.

Thankfully, Jenna remembered nothing of that night. The liquor had stolen her memories, leaving her with a monster hangover, and him with a Jenna-shaped hole in his heart.

"Well?" Megan pressed. "Are you going to tell me? Or do I have to guess?"

"I blew off a friend."

"Yeah? That probably won't score you points in the Friend of the Year competition, but it doesn't sound too dire. Unless you were the best man and blew off the wedding? Left someone stranded at the side of the road somewhere in West Texas? Or promised to feed their cat and totally forgot? Oh, God. Please tell me you didn't kill Fluffy."

He bit back a laugh, feeling slightly better. "A friend came in tonight, and I feel like a complete shit for not meeting her plane."

"Well, there are taxis. And I assume she's an adult?"

"She is, and another friend is there to pick her up."

"I see," she said, and the way she slowly nodded suggested that she saw too much. "I'm guessing that *friend* means *girlfriend*? Or, no. You wouldn't do that. So she must be an ex."

"Really not," he assured her. "Just a friend. Lifelong, since sixth grade."

"Oh, I get it. Longtime friend. High expectations. She's going to be pissed."

"Nah. She's cool. Besides, she knows I usually work nights."

"Then what's the problem?"

He ran his hand over his shaved head, the bristles from the day's growth like sandpaper against his palm. "Hell if I know," he lied, then forced a smile, because whether his problem was guilt or lust or just plain stupidity, she hardly deserved to be on the receiving end of his bullshit.

He rattled his car keys. "How about I buy you one last drink before I take you home?"

"You're sure you don't mind a working drink?" Reece asked as he helped Megan out of his cherished baby blue vintage Chevy pickup. "Normally I wouldn't take you to my job, but we just hired a new bar back, and I want to see how it's going."

He'd snagged one of the coveted parking spots on Sixth Street, about a block down from The Fix, and he glanced automatically toward the bar, the glow from the windows relaxing him. He didn't own the place, but it was like a second home to him and had been for one hell of a long time.

"There's a new guy in training, and you're not there? I thought you told me you were the manager?"

"I did, and I am, but Tyree's there. The owner, I mean. He's always on site when someone new is starting. Says it's his job, not mine. Besides,

Sunday's my day off, and Tyree's a stickler for keeping to the schedule."

"Okay, but why are you going then?"

"Honestly? The new guy's my cousin. He'll probably give me shit for checking in on him, but old habits die hard." Michael had been almost four when Vincent died, and the loss of his dad hit him hard. At sixteen, Reece had tried to be stoic, but Uncle Vincent had been like a second father to him, and he'd always thought of Mike as more brother than cousin. Either way, from that day on, he'd made it his job to watch out for the kid.

"Nah, he'll appreciate it," Megan said. "I've got a little sister, and she gripes when I check up on her, but it's all for show. She likes knowing I have her back. And as for getting a drink where you work, I don't mind at all."

As a general rule, late nights on Sunday were dead, both in the bar and on Sixth Street, the popular downtown Austin street that had been a focal point of the city's nightlife for decades. Tonight was no exception. At half-past one in the morning, the street was mostly deserted. Just a few cars moving slowly, their headlights shining toward the west, and a smattering of couples, stumbling and laughing. Probably tourists on their way back to one of the downtown hotels.

It was late April, though, and the spring weather was drawing both locals and tourists. Soon, the area —and the bar—would be bursting at the seams. Even on a slow Sunday night.

Situated just a few blocks down from Congress Avenue, the main downtown artery, The Fix on Sixth attracted a healthy mix of tourists and locals. The bar had existed in one form or another for decades, becoming a local staple, albeit one that had been falling deeper and deeper into disrepair until Tyree had bought the place six years ago and started it on much-needed life support.

"You've never been here before?" Reece asked as he paused in front of the oak and glass doors etched with the bar's familiar logo.

"I only moved downtown last month. I was in Los Angeles before."

The words hit Reece with unexpected force. Jenna had been in LA, and a wave of both longing and regret crashed over him. He should have gone with Brent. What the hell kind of friend was he, punishing Jenna because he couldn't control his own damn libido?

With effort, he forced the thoughts back. He'd already beaten that horse to death.

"Come on," he said, sliding one arm around her shoulder and pulling open the door with his other. "You're going to love it."

He led her inside, breathing in the familiar mix of alcohol, southern cooking, and something indiscernible he liked to think of as the scent of a damn good time. As he expected, the place was mostly empty. There was no live music on Sunday nights, and at less than an hour to closing, there were only three customers in the front room.

"Megan, meet Cameron," Reece said, pulling out a stool for her as he nodded to the bartender in introduction. Down the bar, he saw Griffin Draper, a regular, lift his head, his face obscured by his hoodie, but his attention on Megan as she chatted with Cam about the house wines.

Reece nodded hello, but Griffin turned back to his notebook so smoothly and nonchalantly that Reece wondered if maybe he'd just been staring into space, thinking, and hadn't seen Reece or Megan at all. That was probably the case, actually. Griff wrote a popular podcast that had been turned into an even more popular web series, and when he wasn't recording the dialogue, he was usually writing a script.

"So where's Mike? With Tyree?"

Cameron made a face, looking younger than his twenty-four years. "Tyree's gone."

"You're kidding. Did something happen with Mike?" His cousin was a responsible kid. Surely he hadn't somehow screwed up his first day on the job.

"No, Mike's great." Cam slid a Scotch in front of Reece. "Sharp, quick, hard worker. He went off the clock about an hour ago, though. So you just missed him."

"Tyree shortened his shift?"

Cam shrugged. "Guess so. Was he supposed to be on until closing?"

"Yeah." Reece frowned. "He was. Tyree say why he cut him loose?"

"No, but don't sweat it. Your cousin's fitting right in. Probably just because it's Sunday and slow. " He made a face. "And since Tyree followed him out, guess who's closing for the first time alone."

"So you're in the hot seat, huh? " Reece tried to sound casual. He was standing behind Megan's stool, but now he moved to lean against the bar, hoping his casual posture suggested that he wasn't worried at all. He was, but he didn't want Cam to realize it. Tyree didn't leave employees to close on their own. Not until he'd spent weeks training them.

"I told him I want the weekend assistant manager position. I'm guessing this is his way of seeing how I work under pressure."

"Probably," Reece agreed half-heartedly. "What did he say?"

"Honestly, not much. He took a call in the office, told Mike he could head home, then about fifteen minutes later said he needed to take off, too, and that I was the man for the night."

"Trouble?" Megan asked.

"No. Just chatting up my boy," Reece said, surprised at how casual his voice sounded. Because the scenario had trouble printed all over it. He just wasn't sure what kind of trouble.

He focused again on Cam. "What about the wait-staff?" Normally, Tiffany would be in the main bar taking care of the customers who sat at tables. "He didn't send them home, too, did he?"

"Oh, no," Cam said. "Tiffany and Aly are scheduled to be on until closing, and they're in the back with—"

But his last words were drowned out by a high-pitched squeal of *"You're here!"* and Reece looked up to find Jenna Montgomery—the woman he craved—barreling across the room and flinging herself into his arms.

Meet Damien Stark

Only his passion could set her free…

Release Me
Claim Me
Complete Me
Anchor Me
Lost With Me

Meet Damien Stark in Release Me, *book 1 of the wildly sensual series that's left millions of readers breathless …*

Chapter One

A cool ocean breeze caresses my bare shoulders,

and I shiver, wishing I'd taken my roommate's advice and brought a shawl with me tonight. I arrived in Los Angeles only four days ago, and I haven't yet adjusted to the concept of summer temperatures changing with the setting of the sun. In Dallas, June is hot, July is hotter, and August is hell.

Not so in California, at least not by the beach. LA Lesson Number One: Always carry a sweater if you'll be out after dark.

Of course, I could leave the balcony and go back inside to the party. Mingle with the millionaires. Chat up the celebrities. Gaze dutifully at the paintings. It is a gala art opening, after all, and my boss brought me here to meet and greet and charm and chat. Not to lust over the panorama that is coming alive in front of me. Bloodred clouds bursting against the pale orange sky. Blue-gray waves shimmering with dappled gold.

I press my hands against the balcony rail and lean forward, drawn to the intense, unreachable beauty of the setting sun. I regret that I didn't bring the battered Nikon I've had since high school. Not that it would have fit in my itty-bitty beaded purse. And a bulky camera bag paired with a little black dress is a big, fat fashion no-no.

But this is my very first Pacific Ocean sunset, and I'm determined to document the moment. I pull out my iPhone and snap a picture.

"Almost makes the paintings inside seem redundant, doesn't it?" I recognize the throaty, feminine voice and turn to face Evelyn Dodge, retired actress turned agent turned patron of the arts—and my hostess for the evening.

"I'm so sorry. I know I must look like a giddy tourist, but we don't have sunsets like this in Dallas."

"Don't apologize," she says. "I pay for that view every month when I write the mortgage check. It damn well better be spectacular."

I laugh, immediately more at ease.

"Hiding out?"

"Excuse me?"

"You're Carl's new assistant, right?" she asks, referring to my boss of three days.

"Nikki Fairchild."

"I remember now. Nikki from Texas." She looks me up and down, and I wonder if she's disappointed that I don't have big hair and cowboy boots. "So who does he want you to charm?"

"Charm?" I repeat, as if I don't know exactly what she means.

She cocks a single brow. "Honey, the man would rather walk on burning coals than come to an art show. He's fishing for investors and you're the bait." She makes a rough noise in the back of her throat. "Don't worry. I won't press you to tell me who. And I don't blame you for hiding out. Carl's brilliant, but he's a bit of a prick."

"It's the brilliant part I signed on for," I say, and she barks out a laugh.

The truth is that she's right about me being the bait. "Wear a cocktail dress," Carl had said. "Something flirty."

Seriously? I mean, *Seriously?*

I should have told him to wear his own damn cocktail dress. But I didn't. Because I want this job. I fought to get this job. Carl's company, C-Squared Technologies, successfully launched three web-based products in the last eighteen months. That track record had caught the industry's eye, and Carl had been hailed as a man to watch.

More important from my perspective, that meant he was a man to learn from, and I'd prepared for the job interview with an intensity bordering on obsession. Landing the position had been a huge coup for me. So what if he wanted me to wear something flirty? It was a small price to pay.

Shit.

"I need to get back to being the bait," I say.

"Oh, hell. Now I've gone and made you feel either guilty or self-conscious. Don't be. Let them get liquored up in there first. You catch more flies with alcohol anyway. Trust me. I know."

She's holding a pack of cigarettes, and now she taps one out, then extends the pack to me. I shake my head. I love the smell of tobacco—it reminds me of my grandfather—but actually inhaling the smoke does nothing for me.

"I'm too old and set in my ways to quit," she says. "But God forbid I smoke in my own damn house. I swear, the mob would burn me in effigy. You're not going to start lecturing me on the dangers of secondhand smoke, are you?"

"No," I promise.

"Then how about a light?"

I hold up the itty-bitty purse. "One lipstick, a credit card, my driver's license, and my phone."

"No condom?"

"I didn't think it was that kind of party," I say dryly.

"I knew I liked you." She glances around the balcony. "What the hell kind of party am I throwing if I don't even have one goddamn candle on one goddamn table? Well, fuck it." She puts the unlit cigarette to her mouth and inhales, her eyes closed and her expression rapturous. I can't help but like her. She wears hardly any makeup, in stark contrast to all the other women here tonight, myself included, and her dress is more of a caftan, the batik pattern as interesting as the woman herself.

She's what my mother would call a brassy broad—

loud, large, opinionated, and self-confident. My mother would hate her. I think she's awesome.

She drops the unlit cigarette onto the tile and grinds it with the toe of her shoe. Then she signals to one of the catering staff, a girl dressed all in black and carrying a tray of champagne glasses.

The girl fumbles for a minute with the sliding door that opens onto the balcony, and I imagine those flutes tumbling off, breaking against the hard tile, the scattered shards glittering like a wash of diamonds.

I picture myself bending to snatch up a broken stem. I see the raw edge cutting into the soft flesh at the base of my thumb as I squeeze. I watch myself clutching it tighter, drawing strength from the pain, the way some people might try to extract luck from a rabbit's foot.

The fantasy blurs with memory, jarring me with its potency. It's fast and powerful, and a little disturbing because I haven't needed the pain in a long time, and I don't understand why I'm thinking about it now, when I feel steady and in control.

I am fine, I think. *I am fine, I am fine, I am fine.*

"Take one, honey," Evelyn says easily, holding a flute out to me.

I hesitate, searching her face for signs that my mask has slipped and she's caught a glimpse of my rawness. But her face is clear and genial.

"No, don't you argue," she adds, misinterpreting my hesitation. "I bought a dozen cases and I hate to see good alcohol go to waste. Hell no," she adds when the girl tries to hand her a flute. "I hate the stuff. Get me a vodka. Straight up. Chilled. Four olives. Hurry up, now. Do you want me to dry up like a leaf and float away?"

The girl shakes her head, looking a bit like a twitchy, frightened rabbit. Possibly one that had sacrificed his foot for someone else's good luck.

Evelyn's attention returns to me. "So how do you like LA? What have you seen? Where have you been? Have you bought a map of the stars yet? Dear God, tell me you're not getting sucked into all that tourist bullshit."

"Mostly I've seen miles of freeway and the inside of my apartment."

"Well, that's just sad. Makes me even more glad

that Carl dragged your skinny ass all the way out here tonight."

I've put on fifteen welcome pounds since the years when my mother monitored every tiny thing that went in my mouth, and while I'm perfectly happy with my size-eight ass, I wouldn't describe it as skinny. I know Evelyn means it as a compliment, though, and so I smile. "I'm glad he brought me, too. The paintings really are amazing."

"Now don't do that—don't you go sliding into the polite-conversation routine. No, no," she says before I can protest. "I'm sure you mean it. Hell, the paintings are wonderful. But you're getting the flat-eyed look of a girl on her best behavior, and we can't have that. Not when I was getting to know the real you."

"Sorry," I say. "I swear I'm not fading away on you."

Because I genuinely like her, I don't tell her that she's wrong—she hasn't met the real Nikki Fairchild. She's met Social Nikki who, much like Malibu Barbie, comes with a complete set of accessories. In my case, it's not a bikini and a convertible.

Instead, I have the *Elizabeth Fairchild Guide for Social Gatherings*.

My mother's big on rules. She claims it's her Southern upbringing. In my weaker moments, I agree. Mostly, I just think she's a controlling bitch. Since the first time she took me for tea at the Mansion at Turtle Creek in Dallas at age three, I have had the rules drilled into my head. How to walk, how to talk, how to dress. What to eat, how much to drink, what kinds of jokes to tell.

I have it all down, every trick, every nuance, and I wear my practiced pageant smile like armor against the world. The result being that I don't think I could truly be myself at a party even if my life depended on it.

This, however, is not something Evelyn needs to know.

"Where exactly are you living?" she asks.

"Studio City. I'm sharing a condo with my best friend from high school."

"Straight down the 101 for work and then back home again. No wonder you've only seen concrete.

Didn't anyone tell you that you should have taken an apartment on the Westside?"

"Too pricey to go it alone," I admit, and I can tell that my admission surprises her. When I make the effort— like when I'm Social Nikki—I can't help but look like I come from money. Probably because I do. Come from it, that is. But that doesn't mean I brought it with me.

"How old are you?"

"Twenty-four."

Evelyn nods sagely, as if my age reveals some secret about me. "You'll be wanting a place of your own soon enough. You call me when you do and we'll find you someplace with a view. Not as good as this one, of course, but we can manage something better than a freeway on-ramp."

"It's not that bad, I promise."

"Of course it's not," she says in a tone that says the exact opposite. "As for views," she continues, gesturing toward the now-dark ocean and the sky that's starting to bloom with stars, "you're welcome to come back anytime and share mine."

"I might take you up on that," I admit. "I'd love to

bring a decent camera back here and take a shot or two."

"It's an open invitation. I'll provide the wine and you can provide the entertainment. A young woman loose in the city. Will it be a drama? A rom-com? Not a tragedy, I hope. I love a good cry as much as the next woman, but I like you. You need a happy ending."

I tense, but Evelyn doesn't know she's hit a nerve. That's why I moved to LA, after all. New life. New story. New Nikki.

I ramp up the Social Nikki smile and lift my champagne flute. "To happy endings. And to this amazing party. I think I've kept you from it long enough."

"Bullshit," she says. "I'm the one monopolizing you, and we both know it."

We slip back inside, the buzz of alcohol-fueled conversation replacing the soft calm of the ocean.

"The truth is, I'm a terrible hostess. I do what I want, talk to whoever I want, and if my guests feel slighted they can damn well deal with it."

I gape. I can almost hear my mother's cries of horror all the way from Dallas.

"Besides," she continues, "this party isn't supposed to be about me. I put together this little shindig to introduce Blaine and his art to the community. He's the one who should be doing the mingling, not me. I may be fucking him, but I'm not going to baby him."

Evelyn has completely destroyed my image of how a hostess for the not-to-be-missed social event of the weekend is supposed to behave, and I think I'm a little in love with her for that.

"I haven't met Blaine yet. That's him, right?" I point to a tall reed of a man. He is bald, but sports a red goatee. I'm pretty sure it's not his natural color. A small crowd hums around him, like bees drawing nectar from a flower. His outfit is certainly as bright as one.

"That's my little center of attention, all right," Evelyn says. "The man of the hour. Talented, isn't he?" Her hand sweeps out to indicate her massive living room. Every wall is covered with paintings. Except for a few benches, whatever furniture was once in the room has been removed and replaced with easels on which more paintings stand.

I suppose technically they are portraits. The models are nudes, but these aren't like anything you would see in a classical art book. There's something edgy about them. Something provocative and raw. I can tell that they are expertly conceived and carried out, and yet they disturb me, as if they reveal more about the person viewing the portrait than about the painter or the model.

As far as I can tell, I'm the only one with that reaction. Certainly the crowd around Blaine is glowing. I can hear the gushing praise from here.

"I picked a winner with that one," Evelyn says. "But let's see. Who do you want to meet? Rip Carrington and Lyle Tarpin? Those two are guaranteed drama, that's for damn sure, and your roommate will be jealous as hell if you chat them up."

"She will?"

Evelyn's brows arch up. "Rip and Lyle? They've been feuding for weeks." She narrows her eyes at me. "The fiasco about the new season of their sitcom? It's all over the Internet? You really don't know them?"

"Sorry," I say, feeling the need to apologize. "My school schedule was pretty intense. And I'm sure you can imagine what working for Carl is like."

Speaking of …

I glance around, but I don't see my boss anywhere.

"That is one serious gap in your education," Evelyn says. "Culture—and yes, pop culture counts—is just as important as—what did you say you studied?"

"I don't think I mentioned it. But I have a double major in electrical engineering and computer science."

"So you've got brains and beauty. See? That's something else we have in common. Gotta say, though, with an education like that, I don't see why you signed up to be Carl's secretary."

I laugh. "I'm not, I swear. Carl was looking for someone with tech experience to work with him on the business side of things, and I was looking for a job where I could learn the business side. Get my feet wet. I think he was a little hesitant to hire me at first—my skills definitely lean toward tech—but I convinced him I'm a fast learner."

She peers at me. "I smell ambition."

I lift a shoulder in a casual shrug. "It's Los Angeles. Isn't that what this town is all about?"

"Ha! Carl's lucky he's got you. It'll be interesting to see how long he keeps you. But let's see ... who here would intrigue you ...?"

She casts about the room, finally pointing to a fifty-something man holding court in a corner. "That's Charles Maynard," she says. "I've known Charlie for years. Intimidating as hell until you get to know him. But it's worth it. His clients are either celebrities with name recognition or power brokers with more money than God. Either way, he's got all the best stories."

"He's a lawyer?"

"With Bender, Twain & McGuire. Very prestigious firm."

"I know," I say, happy to show that I'm not entirely ignorant, despite not knowing Rip or Lyle. "One of my closest friends works for the firm. He started here but he's in their New York office now."

"Well, come on, then, Texas. I'll introduce you." We take one step in that direction, but then Evelyn stops me. Maynard has pulled out his phone, and is shouting instructions at someone. I catch a few well-placed curses and eye Evelyn sideways. She looks unconcerned "He's a pussycat at heart. Trust me, I've worked with him before. Back in my agenting days, we put together more celebrity biopic deals for our clients than I can count. And we fought to keep a few tell-alls off the screen, too." She shakes her head, as if reliving those glory days, then pats my arm. "Still, we'll wait 'til he calms down a bit. In the meantime, though ..."

She trails off, and the corners of her mouth turn down in a frown as she scans the room again. "I don't think he's here yet, but—oh! Yes! Now *there's* someone you should meet. And if you want to talk views, the house he's building has one that makes my view look like, well, like yours." She points toward the entrance hall, but all I see are bobbing heads and haute couture. "He hardly ever accepts invitations, but we go way back," she says.

I still can't see who she's talking about, but then the crowd parts and I see the man in profile. Goose bumps rise on my arms, but I'm not cold. In fact, I'm suddenly very, very warm.

He's tall and so handsome that the word is almost an insult. But it's more than that. It's not his looks, it's his *presence*. He commands the room simply by being in it, and I realize that Evelyn and I aren't the only ones looking at him. The entire crowd has noticed his arrival. He must feel the weight of all those eyes, and yet the attention doesn't faze him at all. He smiles at the girl with the champagne, takes a glass, and begins to chat casually with a woman who approaches him, a simpering smile stretched across her face.

"Damn that girl," Evelyn says. "She never did bring me my vodka."

But I barely hear her. "Damien Stark," I say. My voice surprises me. It's little more than breath.

Evelyn's brows rise so high I notice the movement in my peripheral vision. "Well, how about that?" she says knowingly. "Looks like I guessed right."

"You did," I admit. "Mr. Stark is just the man I want to see."

I hope you enjoyed the excerpt! Grab your own copy of Release Me … or any of the books in the series now!

Meet Damien Stark

The Original Trilogy
Release Me
Claim Me
Complete Me
And Beyond...
Anchor Me
Lost With Me

Some rave reviews for J. Kenner's sizzling romances...

I just get sucked into these books and can not get enough of this series. They are so well written and as satisfying as each book is they leave you greedy for more. — Goodreads reviewer on *Wicked Torture*

A sizzling, intoxicating, sexy read!!!!! J. Kenner had me devouring Wicked Dirty, the second installment of *Stark World Series* in one sitting. I loved everything about this book from the opening pages to the raw and vulnerable characters. With her sophisticated prose, Kenner created a love story that had the perfect blend of lust, passion, sexual tension, raw emotions and love. - Michelle, Four Chicks Flipping Pages

Wicked Dirty CLAIMED and CONSUMED every ounce of me from the very first page. Mind racing. Pulse pounding. Breaths bated. Feels flowing. Eyes wide in anticipation. Heart beating out of my chest. I felt the current of *Wicked Dirty* flow through me. I was DRUNK on this book that was my fine whiskey, so smooth and spectacular, and could not get enough of this *Wicked Dirty* drink. - Karen Bookalicious Babes Blog

"Sinfully sexy and full of heart. Kenner shines in this second chance, slow burn of a romance. Wicked Grind is the perfect book to kick off your summer."- *K. Bromberg, New York Times bestselling author (on Wicked Grind)*

"J. Kenner never disappoints~her books just get better and better." - *Mom's Guilty Pleasure (on Wicked Grind)*

"I don't think J. Kenner could write a bad story if she tried. ... Wicked Grind is a great beginning to what I'm positive will be a very successful series. ... The line forms here." *iScream Books (On Wicked Grind)*

"Scorching, sweet, and soul-searing, *Anchor Me* is the ultimate love story that stands the test of time and tribulation. THE TRUEST LOVE!" *Bookalicious Babes Blog (on Anchor Me)*

"J. Kenner has brought this couple to life and the character connection that I have to these two holds no bounds and that is testament to J.

Kenner's writing ability." *The Romance Cover (on Anchor Me)*

"J. Kenner writes an emotional and personal story line. ... The premise will captivate your imagination; the characters will break your heart; the romance continues to push the envelope." *The Reading Café (on Anchor Me)*

"Kenner may very well have cornered the market on sinfully attractive, dominant antiheroes and the women who swoon for them . . ." *Romantic Times*

"*Wanted* is another J. Kenner masterpiece . . . This was an intriguing look at self-discovery and forbidden love all wrapped into a neat little action-suspense package. There was plenty of sexual tension and eventually action. Evan was hot, hot, hot! Together, they were combustible. But can we expect anything less from J. Kenner?" *Reading Haven*

"*Wanted* by J. Kenner is the whole package! A toe-curling smokin' hot read, full of incredible characters and a brilliant storyline that you won't be able to get enough of. I can't wait for the next book in this series . . . I'm hooked!" *Flirty & Dirty Book Blog*

"J. Kenner's evocative writing thrillingly captures the power of physical attraction, the pull of longing, the universe-altering effect one person can have on another. . . . *Claim Me* has the emotional depth to back up the sex . . . Every scene is infused with both erotic tension, and the tension of wondering what lies beneath Damicn's veneer – and how and when it will be revealed." *Heroes and Heartbreakers*

"*Claim Me* by J. Kenner is an erotic, sexy and exciting ride. The story between Damien and Nikki is amazing and written beautifully. The intimate and detailed sex scenes will leave you fanning yourself to cool down. With the writing style of Ms. Kenner you almost feel like you are there in the story riding along the emotional rollercoaster with Damien and Nikki." *Fresh Fiction*

"PERFECT for fans of *Fifty Shades of Grey* and *Bared to You*. *Release Me* is a powerful and erotic romance novel that is sure to make adult romance readers sweat, sigh and swoon." *Reading, Eating & Dreaming Blog*

"I will admit, I am in the 'I loved *Fifty Shades*' camp,

but after reading *Release Me*, Mr. Grey only scratches the surface compared to Damien Stark." *Cocktails and Books Blog*

"It is not often when a book is so amazingly well-written that I find it hard to even begin to accurately describe it . . . I recommend this book to everyone who is interested in a passionate love story." *Romancebookworm's Reviews*

"The story is one that will rank up with the *Fifty Shades* and Cross Fire trilogies." *Incubus Publishing Blog*

"The plot is complex, the characters engaging, and J. Kenner's passionate writing brings it all perfectly together." *Harlequin Junkie*

Also by J. Kenner

The Stark Saga Novels:

Only his passion could set her free…

Meet Damien Stark

The Original Trilogy

Release Me

Claim Me

Complete Me

And Beyond…

Anchor Me

Lost With Me

Stark Ever After

(Stark Saga novellas):

Happily ever after is just the beginning.

The passion between Damien & Nikki continues.

Take Me

Have Me

Play My Game

Seduce Me

Unwrap Me

Deepest Kiss

Entice Me

Hold Me

Please Me

The Steele Books/Stark International:

He was the only man who made her feel alive.

Say My Name

On My Knees

Under My Skin

Take My Dare (includes short story Steal My Heart)

Stark International Novellas:

Meet Jamie & Ryan-so hot it sizzles.

Tame Me

Tempt Me

S.I.N. Trilogy:

It was wrong for them to be together…

…but harder to stay apart.

Dirtiest Secret

Hottest Mess

Sweetest Taboo

Stand alone novels:

Most Wanted:

Three powerful, dangerous men.

Three sensual, seductive women.

Wanted

Heated

Ignited

Wicked Nights (Stark World):

Sometimes it feels so damn good to be bad.

Wicked Grind

Wicked Dirty

Wicked Torture

Man of the Month

Who's your man of the month …?

Down On Me

Hold On Tight

Need You Now

Start Me Up

Get It On

In Your Eyes

Turn Me On

Shake It Up

All Night Long

In Too Deep

Light My Fire

Walk The Line

Bar Bites: A Man of the Month Cookbook(by J. Kenner
& Suzanne M. Johnson)

Additional Titles

Wild Thing

One Night (A Stark World short story in the Second
Chances anthology)

Also by Julie Kenner

The Protector (Superhero) Series:

The Cat's Fancy (prequel)

Aphrodite's Kiss

Aphrodite's Passion

Aphrodite's Secret

Aphrodite's Flame

Aphrodite's Embrace (novella)

Aphrodite's Delight (novella – free download)

Demon Hunting Soccer Mom Series:

Carpe Demon

California Demon

Demons Are Forever

Deja Demon

The Demon You Know (short story)

Demon Ex Machina

Pax Demonica

Day of the Demon

The Dark Pleasures Series:

Caress of Darkness

Find Me In Darkness

Find Me In Pleasure

Find Me In Passion

Caress of Pleasure

The Blood Lily Chronicles:

Tainted

Torn

Turned

Rising Storm:

Rising Storm: Tempest Rising

Rising Storm: Quiet Storm

Devil May Care:

Seducing Sin

Tempting Fate

About the Author

J. Kenner (aka Julie Kenner) is the *New York Times*, *USA Today*, *Publishers Weekly*, *Wall Street Journal* and #1 International bestselling author of over one hundred novels, novellas and short stories in a variety of genres.

JK has been praised by *Publishers Weekly* as an author with a "flair for dialogue and eccentric characterizations" and by *RT Bookclub* for having "cornered the market on sinfully attractive, dominant antiheroes and the women who swoon for them." A six-time finalist for Romance Writers of America's prestigious RITA award, JK took home the first RITA trophy awarded in the category of erotic romance in 2014 for her novel, *Claim Me* (book 2 of her Stark Trilogy).

In her previous career as an attorney, JK worked as a lawyer in Southern California and Texas. She currently lives in Central Texas, with her husband, two daughters, and two rather spastic cats.

More ways to connect:
www.jkenner.com
Text JKenner to 21000 for JK's text alerts.

facebook.com/jkennerbooks

twitter.com/juliekenner